PRAISE FOR M. L. BUCHMAN

3x "Top 10 Romance of the Year"

— BOOKLIST

13 times "Top Pick of the Month"

— NIGHT OWL REVIEWS

I became completely immersed in this story and it had me at page one. Entertaining and full of emotion.

— FRESH FICTION, *WHERE DREAMS ARE BORN*

A favorite author of mine. I'll read anything that carries his name, no questions asked. Meet your new favorite author!

— THE SASSY BOOKSTER, *FLASH OF FIRE*

M.L. Buchman is guaranteed to get me lost in a good story.

— THE READING CAFE, *WAY OF THE WARRIOR: NSDQ*

I love Buchman's writing. His vivid descriptions bring everything to life in an unforgettable way.

— PURE JONEL, *HOT POINT*

Buchman has catapulted his way to the top tier of my favorite authors.

— FRESH FICTION

The only thing you'll ask yourself is, "When does the next one come out?"

— *WAIT UNTIL MIDNIGHT*, RT REVIEWS, 4 STARS

Superb! Miranda is utterly compelling!

— *BOOKLIST,* STARRED REVIEW

Miranda Chase continues to astound and charm.

— BARB M.

Escape Rating: A. Five Stars! OMG just start with *Drone* and be prepared for a fantastic binge-read!

— READING REALITY

WHERE DREAMS ARE OF CHRISTMAS
A PIKE PLACE MARKET SEATTLE ROMANCE

M. L. BUCHMAN

Copyright 2017 Matthew Lieber Buchman

New Cover 2021

Published by Buchman Bookworks, Inc.

All rights reserved.

This book, or parts thereof, may not be reproduced in any form without permission from the author.

Receive a free Starter Library and discover more by this author at: www.mlbuchman.com

Cover Design: Melody Barber

Cover images:

Married couple sat face to face on sofa © photography33

Composite image of christmas tree on white background © Wavebreakmedia

SIGN UP FOR M. L. BUCHMAN'S NEWSLETTER TODAY

and receive:
Release News
Free Short Stories
a Free Starter Anthology

Do it today. Do it now.
www.mlbuchman.com/newsletter

Other works by M. L. Buchman: *(* - also in audio)*

Action-Adventure Thrillers

Dead Chef
One Chef!
Two Chef!

Miranda Chase
Drone*
Thunderbolt*
Condor*
Ghostrider*
Raider*
Chinook*
Havoc*
White Top*

Romantic Suspense

Delta Force
Target Engaged*
Heart Strike*
Wild Justice*
Midnight Trust*

Firehawks
Main Flight
Pure Heat
Full Blaze
Hot Point*
Flash of Fire*
Wild Fire

Smokejumpers
Wildfire at Dawn*
Wildfire at Larch Creek*
Wildfire on the Skagit*

The Night Stalkers
Main Flight
The Night Is Mine
I Own the Dawn
Wait Until Dark
Take Over at Midnight

Light Up the Night
Bring On the Dusk
By Break of Day

and the Navy
Christmas at Steel Beach
Christmas at Peleliu Cove

White House Holiday
Daniel's Christmas*
Frank's Independence Day*
Peter's Christmas*
Zachary's Christmas*
Roy's Independence Day*
Damien's Christmas*

5E
Target of the Heart
Target Lock on Love
Target of Mine
Target of One's Own

Shadow Force: Psi
At the Slightest Sound*
At the Quietest Word*
At the Merest Glance*
At the Clearest Sensation*

White House Protection Force
Off the Leash*
On Your Mark*
In the Weeds*

Contemporary Romance

Eagle Cove
Return to Eagle Cove
Recipe for Eagle Cove
Longing for Eagle Cove
Keepsake for Eagle Cove

Henderson's Ranch
Nathan's Big Sky*
Big Sky, Loyal Heart*
Big Sky Dog Whisperer*

Other works by M. L. Buchman:

Contemporary Romance (cont)

Love Abroad
Heart of the Cotswolds: England
Path of Love: Cinque Terre, Italy

Where Dreams
Where Dreams are Born
Where Dreams Reside
Where Dreams Are of Christmas*
Where Dreams Unfold
Where Dreams Are Written
Where Dreams Continue

Science Fiction / Fantasy

Deities Anonymous
Cookbook from Hell: Reheated
Saviors 101

Single Titles
The Nara Reaction
Monk's Maze
the Me and Elsie Chronicles

Non-Fiction

Strategies for Success
Managing Your Inner Artist/Writer
Estate Planning for Authors*
Character Voice
Narrate and Record Your Own Audiobook*

Short Story Series by M. L. Buchman:

Romantic Suspense

Antarctic Ice Fliers

Delta Force
Th Delta Force Shooters
The Delta Force Warriors

Firehawks
The Firehawks Lookouts
The Firehawks Hotshots
The Firebirds

The Night Stalkers
The Night Stalkers 5D Stories
The Night Stalkers 5E Stories
The Night Stalkers CSAR
The Night Stalkers Wedding Stories

US Coast Guard

White House Protection Force

Contemporary Romance

Eagle Cove

Henderson's Ranch*

Where Dreams

Action-Adventure Thrillers

Dead Chef

Miranda Chase Origin Stories

Science Fiction / Fantasy

Deities Anonymous

Other
The Future Night Stalkers
Single Titles

ABOUT THIS TITLE

A foodie Christmas romance in Seattle! The best time for two hearts to awaken to life's possibilities!

Maria Amelia Avico Parrano *is beloved by all: her son, his restaurant staff, and the people drawn to her love of life and Italian pastries in the heart of Seattle's Pike Place Market. After years of warming the hearts of others, Maria wants to cook up a little heat for herself.*

Hogan Stanford *watches the world pass by far below his hi-rise condo. The merest glimpse of Maria draws him back to life again. Basking in her bright light, he learns there's more to life than he ever imagined.*

Hogan offers his heart. Now Maria must decide if she can trust hers.

CHAPTER 1

*M*aria Amelia Avico Parrano sat down inside the take-out window of her son's restaurant. She loved watching the slow mornings of Post Alley in the heart of Seattle's Pike Place Market. She'd already spent several hours baking but for most, the day was barely begun.

Behind her, the restaurant was still quiet. Angelo's Tuscan Hearth wouldn't open until lunch. Already, her Angelo had slid the morning's produce and protein purchases into the walk-in fridge and gone to the gym for his morning workout. The first prep chef wouldn't arrive for another hour. For now, the restaurant was all hers.

Her new life astounded her.

Six months ago, the couple she'd served for the last three decades in New York had retired and didn't need a resident chef anymore. They had rewarded her most comfortably for her years of service and now she had a place here at her son's restaurant on the other side of the country.

Here, too, she had met new friends and saw her son and his fiancée every day. How could a woman not smile when every morning was such a miracle?

Retired comfortably at forty-seven; that change made no sense at all. She wanted to thank Angelo every day for giving her a purpose. She didn't, of course. It wouldn't do for him to become too pleased with himself, even if he was the becoming acknowledged as the best Italian chef in all of America.

It was time.

She flicked on the heater switch; in moments a warm wash of air blew onto her legs. When she slid up the kitchen window to face the chill first day of December, the cold wasn't too harsh. Russell, her former employer's son and her son's best friend, had installed another heater over the outside of the window to radiate a wall of warmth down onto the customers and an awning to keep Seattle's December rains at bay.

Russell was such a sweet man, she really didn't need that much protection. But she had helped raise both Angelo and Russell, so of course they saw her as old and frail. That was their role in life. Youth was supposed to think that way. But she didn't feel that way. Not even a little.

Besides, she had far too much fun selling coffee and pastries at her take-out window to stop merely because of the weather. Already some of her regulars were loitering on the wet brickwork of Post Alley and quickly huddled around the window as soon as she opened it.

"Good morning, Maria." The near chorus was music to her ears.

"*Buongiorno,* Clara, Joseph, and William. I do no see you as much as I do when the weather is nice. Don't you love your Maria anymore?" She handed William his cappuccino first to soften the tease. He dropped a five-dollar bill in the jar she'd set out. She'd made a decorative tile with "Breakfast $3" worked in lavender against a yellow glaze at one of those paint-it-yourself pottery places. "The price," she would tell people, "she is fixed in stone." Then she gave William a fresh *cornetto.*

"What's in it this morning?" he took a big bite without

waiting for an answer. "Oh my God!" He managed to mumble with his mouth full, a smile on his face, and crumbs clustering on the lapels of his sharp lawyer's suit.

"I make special for you a sweet *Prosciutto di San Daniele* with a fresh, tangy *Robiola Bosina* cheese." Her breakfasts weren't intended to make money, they were to entice people into her son's restaurant. She also enjoyed the social time after her quiet morning working alone.

Clara bit into hers and closed her eyes, as usual, to relish the tastes. Joseph went for the cappuccino first, still looking more asleep than awake. Other regulars had queued up as they paid and chatted, only moving to the edge of the awning and the radiant heat as others pressed inward.

Soon the milling, happy crowd of locals attracted passing tourists. Inside of five minutes there were more people that she didn't recognize than ones that she did.

Henry came over from the fish market and she refused his money, as she had a hundred times before, but he always offered. Henry always held back the best of the day's catch for Angelo or his *sous chef* Manuel each morning, today it was the black sea bass.

"Maria, when are you going to marry me?"

"I could never marry you, Henry. You always smell of fish. I could no marry such a man." He of course knew that was a little joke. His fish were always so fresh and he kept everything so clean. He was a vendor, and a very smart one, not a fisherman.

"I'll give it all up for you." He flashed her one of his smiles.

She was half tempted to at least date him. He was such a nice man, and good looking, even if a bit round in the belly. His graying hair would go silver and make him a very handsome older man. But, though she liked him, there was no spark.

Maria wanted spark. She wanted electricity. Lightning bolts! All the time as a single mother raising her boy—boys because, growing up, Russell had been underfoot in her kitchen as much as her son—she'd only dated a few times. Now Maria could only hope that she hadn't waited too long and missed her chance.

She served and chatted with a dozen more tourists after Henry left. Her son had found lightning in Jo Thompson. And Russell in Cassidy. The two boys were so sweet in love that it was hard to credit that they were men grown, always doting on their women while trying desperately to appear the strong men they couldn't help being if they tried.

Jo and Cassidy, were both such exceedingly competent women, they made her feel out of her depth. All she had ever done was cook and raise the two boys.

But she'd felt that spark once in her life. She'd felt it right to the very core of her being. A love for a no-good, useless man who had walked away after taking her virginity and leaving her pregnant with a son. Maria had been forced to come to America to hide the shameful pregnancy of an unmarried Italian Roman Catholic girl. She'd never gone back to Manarola for more than to visit.

She wanted that fire. She wanted someone who made her blood burn and her heart race. Each morning for an hour, perhaps two, she smiled and teased and enjoyed herself immensely. It had become her contribution to her son's success. He was the great chef, but she knew how to charm the people.

The morning always went too quickly; another dozen *cornetti* and she'd be sold out for the day. She made her usual bet with herself. Today she guessed that nine, perhaps ten of the people she'd served would be back for an Italian lunch when the restaurant opened. Even one additional customer would pay for the minor loss she cost the restaurant with each day's breakfast service.

She served a young Chinese couple who didn't speak a word of English, or Italian either. It didn't matter. She helped them figure out which bill to put in the jar and they left ready to explore the waterfront with their cappuccinos and *cornetti* in hand.

A man drifted to the take-out counter window during a momentary lull.

Maria Amelia recognized him. Lately, he'd often wandered by in the mornings, slowing down but never stopping. He always appeared to want to, but never quite managed.

Her greeting elicited little more than a friendly nod. A shy one. He wore old sneakers with white socks, dark-brown khakis that had started to fray where the hems scuffed along the ground, a red flannel shirt under a faded jeans jacket, and a baseball cap with some computer-looking logo. The whole outfit had clearly been worn several years too long, probably from a Goodwill store.

He didn't have a beard, but very much needed a shave. It was long enough she could see it would have a little salt in the pepper if he let it grow.

For all that he was quite the handsomest man she had served that morning. Not the prettiest, so many of the young men were pretty. Those fresh clean faces that thought they knew all of the world while having seen none of it.

This man had seen much of it. Perhaps too much, perhaps not, but it showed on his solid features and in the soft brown eyes that didn't skitter aside despite his unease, or downward despite her low-cut dress. She wouldn't mind much if they did, after all, why was a woman built the way she was if not to share it a little bit? But she liked that he didn't stare.

He stopped uncertainly several steps from her window, just at the point where she could see the rain dripping off the awning, splashing onto the brim of his hat, and trickling off the brim and into his open jacket.

The man pulled out a wallet, made a back-and-forth motion with his fingers as if searching for money, then shoved it back in his pocket.

As he turned away, Maria called to him.

"Don't go."

He stopped, this time with the drip falling down the back of his neck. When he turned back at her, his nice eyes looked just a little wild. Fear that he couldn't afford to pay even so little for a breakfast.

"Here, it is my last. You should have it." She held out a *cornetto* and cappuccino.

He hesitated, so shy it was almost painful to watch.

"I always save the best for last. So these must be for you."

The man came and took them, careful not to touch her as he did so. His nails needed trimming, but the hands were good ones. He didn't use them for manual labor, but they showed a man who had used them for more than office work his whole life. A few small burns and nicks she recognized as someone who cooked, and wasn't particularly good at it, which only made her like him all the more.

He almost managed a smile before turning away and hurrying into the rain.

HIS CHEEKS BURNING WITH SHAME, Hogan Stanford hurried down Pike Place Market's Post Alley until he was out of sight of Maria's window. Then he circled around to the antiques place at the corner of Post and Stewart and peeked back toward Angelo's Tuscan Hearth.

It was a gray, drizzling December morning, freezing water was trickling down his back, and he was a complete and total idiot.

He hadn't been able to say a word.

He'd first noticed her from his condo's window which faced Puget Sound.

Or he liked to think it was her even though it was impossible.

From his twelfth-floor condo, he had the perfect place to watch the tourists mob up and down the four short, bricked blocks of Pike Place Market. It had become one of his favorite pastimes. Even if he didn't like to join the fray, it always seemed so full of life.

And in the midst of it all there had been a flash of color, of sky-blue coat and golden hat that had glittered in the crowd. There had been a liveliness to the tourist's stroll that had captured his imagination.

That was what had finally drawn him outdoors to wander the streets of the Pike Place Market rather than his usual mode of watching from safe behind his window. Even the slightest chance of seeing her again, but he never saw her again. He wasn't even sure it had *been* a woman—a flash of color and life, then gone.

A week later, he'd spotted another woman, striding purposefully through the market. She had that same…brilliance. Like sunshine.

She wore a light gray jacket on the warm winter day. Dressed in a red skirt, a vivid orange blouse, and a sunny yellow kerchief over her dark, curling hair, she'd looked like a flower in bloom. It should be impossible that there were two women in the world like that, but there must be.

He'd been so stunned by her beauty that he'd lost track of her when she must've ducked into a store. It took him another week to spot her again, though at least now he had a face to go by. This time she sat in the window at Angelo's Tuscan Hearth Ristorante, framed by the wood-and-brick window frame, like a Botticelli.

Today she'd been dressed in brilliant blues as she served up breakfast and charm in equal portions. She embodied a ray of sunshine in an otherwise murky world on this dreary December day. At least he was fairly sure it was December now.

He peeked again around the brickwork corner and back up Post Alley. She was bantering happily with another customer. Leaning her elbow on the counter and resting her chin on her hand, she looked as if she could happily visit away the whole morning.

It was an ability Hogan had never understood.

He didn't know whether to be impressed by how natural she was, or be nervous that she would talk everyone to death and be a bore. Yet she never appeared to bore anyone, though he had watched her many times. He decided that she had an uncanny awareness of the mood of each individual she met.

Hogan noted with some chagrin that she served the woman a *cornetto* and a paper cup. The one still warm in his hands hadn't been her last after all. Thinking him homeless, she said it to make him feel less embarrassed. People were never that nice. It had to be an act…but again, it didn't feel like one.

Being stupid, Hogan. It was one of his trademarks, but he couldn't approach her. Half a dozen times over the few weeks since he'd spotted her, he'd walked by while she was serving, trying to work up the nerve. Finally this morning he'd managed it.

Now she slid her window down. In moments, the soft red glow of the overhead heater faded to black. Finally sold out. He shifted back around the corner and out of sight of the restaurant, then rested his back against the wet brick. The moisture slowly seeped through at his shoulders and butt.

She was so different from the dark and brooding Vera who had totally screwed up his life.

He knew he had to get out and speak to someone. All he'd wanted was one moment in the glow of a woman as bright and cheerful as the one in the restaurant window.

And then he'd looked in his wallet and realized that the smallest bill he was carrying was a hundred.

Then she'd decided he was homeless.

How sad was that?

And he'd let her think it.

Really sad, he answered his own question, knowing it was absolutely true.

CHAPTER 2

*H*ogan had two places to be, which was an improvement. For the first six months, he'd only had the one, his condo. His buddies—his buddy, he'd chased off pretty much everyone except Eric by being Mister Gloom for so long, had insisted that he get out. There was only so long you could hole up in a condo at the heart of a city as alive as Seattle.

So, now he either sat watching at his condo's window a dozen stories into the sky above the world of the Pike Place Market. Or he wandered the half mile down to the Lawrence Armed Forces Shelter in Pioneer Square.

He wasn't a vet, but Eric Lawrence didn't hold it against him, though some of the guys had at first. Now that he'd shown up every afternoon for a month they were starting to forgive him for never having served. He'd spent his twenties fighting computer code and corporate politics, a far less lethal environment. He'd loved doing it, but now he was mid-forties, financially set for life, and he was done. Corporate wars had taken the fun out of it.

The guys at the shelter let Hogan work in the kitchen and keep to himself. Mostly.

Richie was in rare form today and clearly his PTSD needed a target. As usual, Hogan was it.

"Hogan, man," all of Richie's diatribes started that way. On days like this he couldn't just chop vegetables and leave Hogan in peace. Each time it was something different. Richie had lost all connection to normal but seemed to keep hunting around looking for it, hoping someday he'd hit it by chance.

"Hogan, man, I can't believe you never even shot anybody."

Today wasn't going to be the day.

"You don't know what you can really do until then."

Hogan, kept his focus on the chowder kettle. It was an exceptional device, absolutely suited to one purpose, making large batches of soup quickly. To make the chowder, it took two large number ten cans of condensed chowder, that came out in a near solid, brownish mass, filled with a thousand bits of white potato, and gray clams. Even the green flecks of parsley were included. Add two gallons of milk and set the timer for twenty minutes. The steam-jacketed kettle heated it through without scorching, as long as he remembered to stir it and scrape the bottom every five minutes. A long handle then let you tip the contents right into the serving inserts for the steam table. He liked the efficiency and single mindedness of it.

A trait it shared with Richie. The man was starting in on the different methods of killing the enemy that he had supposedly experienced. To hear him talk, he had won Desert Storm single-handedly back in the '90s and been at the shelter ever since. Even Eric didn't know how much of Richie was real and how much came from his primary hobby, collecting war movies. He claimed it was the only thing that kept him calm, the sound of war a constant in the background.

Richie was the most extreme person in the kitchen. There was room for five of them. Richie and Sam worked at a long steel table. Today they were filleting great tubs of cleaned fish, wielding long curved knives as if they were extensions of their arms. The fish flew into stacks, neat little butterflied pieces just perfect for making the fish and chips for tonight. Standard Friday fare.

His friend Eric was at the dishwasher and his wife Betsy worked battering and breading the fish as fast as the other two men sliced it up. Eric had had an easy tour, but none of the three friends who'd signed up when he did had come home. So, he paid back his missing friends by founding the kitchen.

He'd recruited Hogan just recently. They'd met at a bookstore and both reached for the last copy of the new Clive Cussler book at the same time. That was all the opening Eric needed, ever. When he'd learned Hogan was at loose ends, he'd dragged him down to the shelter, "Until he found something better to do." After a month, Hogan hadn't found anything better. And the work at the shelter was becoming more important to him, helping out, making a difference, even if it was a small one.

Hogan began chopping the heads of lettuce and throwing them in the big tubs of water to stay fresh. Cans of beans, beets, and a half dozen other items would be opened right before service to set up the salad bar. Then a half-dozen chilled onions to slice up thin.

He wished Richie would stop saying, "Hogan, man" so that he could think about Maria. He'd heard someone call her that one day. The fishmonger, in his big voice shouting to her, "Maria, my love. You must run away with me." Her laugh had sparkled and lit the rainy day as if it had struck fire and rainbows.

That was a good metaphor for her. Fire and rainbows, heat and life, vibrant and multi-spectral.

He wondered if she smelled as good as her kitchen.

That's when he noticed the smell in this kitchen. He rushed

to the chowder pot. Scorched. The chowder would be fine, but it would take him an extra half hour today to get it clean.

Not that he had anything better to do.

CHAPTER 3

*I*nside, the bang and clatter of the lunch-service prep crews filled the restaurant's kitchen.

Manuel, Angelo's *sous chef,* was pushing his new assistant Nora to see if he could make her panic. Maria smiled to herself, no luck yet.

Luisa and Graziella were rehearsing the new menu items for the daily fresh sheet. "Black sea bass poached in a Piemonte Roero Arneis, that's a slightly sweet white wine of northern Italy, with a rub of basil…"

Maria let the words drift into the background. The fish would be served with a surprise pairing of a young Barbaresco red, it would be an innovative pleasure on the palate. The other noises were starting to sound so familiar; it was if she'd never been anywhere else.

"Mama!"

"Angelo!" Her tone, as strident as his, brought him to a halt. "What you got to yell for?"

Her son blushed. A grown man of thirty, newly engaged, and a successful restaurateur and she could still make him blush. He was so sweet. It made her feel all motherly inside. It also made her feel old, and she didn't like that at all.

"Now," she took him by the hand and led him over to the stainless-steel prep table to one side of the kitchen. The tubs of the iced black sea bass filled one end. A big wheel of Parmigiano-Reggiano cheese, dusky inside its thick rind and ready for breakdown, sat on the other.

He followed her reluctantly, but she was firm. The last thing Nora or Manuel needed during their lunch preparations was whatever had upset her son.

Then she spotted the newspaper in his hand and she suspected that she knew. She pushed him onto one of the stools and pulled another from under the table for herself. There was the dough for a new puff pastry she was developing that would need tending shortly, but it could wait five, perhaps ten minutes.

"Sit like a good boy. Manuel," she called over to Angelo's head chef, "could you please make a bowl of pasta for us. Use Nora's nice Bolognese."

"It's not ready yet," he grumbled even as he made two plates and brought them over.

"Yes it is, Manuel. Now you no more plaguing the sweet girl and tell her that she is doing so very fine. Before she make herself sick with worry that she is no good enough."

He winked at her and offered the sly grin that so rarely creased his handsome Mexican features. The fact that he was the best Italian chef she'd ever met, after her son of course, was only one of life's little oddities that she so enjoyed.

"Don't you wink at me, young man. You go tell Nora that she is doing wonderful or I tell her that you are sweet on her whether or not you are."

He blanched, "No, I—" Then his tongue tied into a knot just as Graziella breezed into the kitchen with the day's first orders. Now wasn't that interesting.

Manuel wisely retreated, a quick glance showed that her son had missed his chef's reaction to the queen of the front of house. They would make such a beautiful couple. Manuel's dark complexion reflected his Oaxacan heritage and Graziella glowed just as richly with the shade of the Mediterranean. His square features and broad shoulders were in sharp contrast to her slender build. Both had black hair, his short and curled, and hers was a man's dream, often in a thick braid, at other times free and floating along behind her. She was taller, but Manuel didn't appear to mind.

Yes, they would make a beautiful couple, though she would worry about that later. At the moment she had to worry about her son and her puff pastry, in that order. And neither would wait long.

"Mama," Angelo laid the paper down beside his pasta bowl. A circle around one of the ads on the personals page. Yes, that was it.

"Why do you read such things," she waved a fork of Nora's pasta Bolognese in the paper's general direction before tasting it. Oh, it was so good. "You are a married boy. You should not be reading such thing as personal ads."

"I'm not married yet, I'm engaged. And I didn't."

"Then why are you in here complaining?"

"Mama! Henry read it and asked if that could possibly be my mama? I read the ad and what was I to think?"

She hadn't really counted on Henry the fishmonger reading it. He was a little too pushy about being in love with her and she had decided definitely no. She also hadn't planned on her son reading it. So simple an ad. Too simple maybe.

Very Italian cook, SWF, 47 seeks friend(s).
Person to laugh with, dance with, and dine with.
Believes in friends, family, and herself.

"Of course I told him it wasn't you. Why would my beautiful mama have to advertise for friends? She is already friends with everyone." Angelo squinted down at the ad then looked back up at her. "It isn't you, is it?"

Maria thought about how it felt. Yes, she knew everybody, their names and those of their wives and children. But how could she possibly explain it to someone like her son? His best friend Russell lived only a few blocks away. Angelo had moved from his condo in Pioneer Square to live with his beautiful Jo in her high-rise condo in the heart of Seattle looking down at Lake Union and out at the Olympic mountains.

Where did that leave her? She had been in Seattle six months now. She came in early, as a good Italian *pâtissier* had to for her pastry to be perfect and her breads to rise. And by mid-afternoon, she was done for the day. She often stayed through dinner, because she had nothing more to do. Going to sit alone in Angelo's condo in Pioneer Square was not satisfying, and she didn't like to sit by herself at movies or plays. Or restaurants for that matter.

She liked people, but who in Seattle did she really know? No one except her two boys, Angelo and his everything-but-birth brother, Russell. It was a good soup, but it had no spice.

She refocused on Angelo's questioning gaze. Some questions, she decided were not to be answered. Time to give him something else to worry about and then go fold her puff pastry dough.

Maria patted him reassuringly on the cheek which he interpreted exactly as she meant him to. Then had a though of how to distract him as she collected their empty bowls.

"So, my boy," she whispered, "Manuel and Graziella. What do you think? Their children would be so very pretty."

HOGAN STANFORD LEFT the Lawrence Armed Forces Shelter kitchen later than usual. Eric Lawrence had decided on the name for two reasons. First, it kept the riffraff out. It was a clear sign that said, "There are messed up military dudes in here. If you aren't one, stay away."

The other shelters had so appreciated having so many of the street's hardcases have somewhere else to go, that they'd done everything they could in Eric's rough-start first year.

The second benefit had been that the guys, and the one or two really messed up women, understood each other and were better at dealing with each other's oddities. They'd get into arguments between which force was better or which war tougher, but someone always stepped in when things got too heated. They were like an engine, a really screwed up one that really shouldn't still be running, but it seemed to work despite all of its problems.

By the time Hogan had scrubbed the chowder pot, Richie had been in full meltdown-recovery. In some ways that was even worse. He'd cornered Hogan for a half hour to apologize for being a jerk and to spin out yet another personal story, one that sounded suspiciously like a John Wayne plot. Though Hogan now knew better than to point that out.

When all was said and done, he'd practically crawled out the kitchen door and turned up First Avenue to head back up to his place overlooking Pike Place Market. It had been a good shift, he'd helped put food into a lot of tired vets with cold bellies, but he was exhausted.

He'd planned on hitting one of the banks to break one of his hundred-dollar bills so that he could buy breakfast tomorrow. He'd pay with a ten, to pay Maria back for her kindness today. Or would that be rude? It didn't matter, it was too late anyway. Between Richie and the chowder pot, they'd made him miss the end of the banking hours. And her window would be closed before the banks opened in the morning.

He hadn't gone ten steps into the cold darkness of a Northwest evening when he practically ran someone down. He mumbled an, "Oh sorry, just distracted I guess," and made to move on when a hand on his coat sleeve stopped him.

He looked up, startled, into the dark eyes of Maria… He didn't even know her last name. They hadn't been this close this morning. Now they stood mere inches apart. Barely up to his chin in height, she looked up at him.

Her eyes weren't just dark, even in the early evening streetlights they were rich brown, like warm chocolate that somehow sparkled, almost the same color as the lock of her hair that poked out around a bright blue scarf.

His first impression that her face was worthy of a Botticelli painting was powerfully reinforced. She reminded him of the one he'd seen in Florence. Maria was a darker-skinned Venus, observing an Allegory of Spring. Her heavy coat of good brown leather, hugged her frame. He knew from seeing her in the window these last mornings, that Maria had glorious curves and a trim waist.

He also knew that he was staring at her far beyond what was appropriate for their casual meeting. "Run," he advised her. At least he thought the recommendation loudly. Any woman with the least common sense would know to run away from him, but she remained.

"Did they give you enough to eat?"

"Huh?" That was the best answer he could manage. What was she…

"The shelter. Did they give you enough to eat?"

He glanced over his shoulder. The Lawrence Shelter lay not a dozen paces behind him, she must have seen him exit the kitchen door.

"No. Yes. I…" He never ate there, because he wanted as much food as possible to go to the men. Eric offered him free meals, but he said it was part of his contribution. He'd planned to go home and maybe cook a hamburger or some chicken. Maybe it was an order-out-Chinese night?

"They serve plenty there. Eric does an excellent job."

Maria nodded. "Too bad you've already eaten. I would make offer to you to make a home-cooked meal. I do not much enjoy eating alone. Well, have a good night."

He turned to say something as she walked away, anything. He found no words.

"And tomorrow," she spoke over her shoulder. "You come back to the window at Angelo's, I make sure you have a good breakfast."

Then she was gone.

Hogan could have felt dumber, he just didn't know how.

He stood at the heart of Pioneer Square so long that a chill finally found its way in to shiver up his spine. The small triangular park that was the heart of the square was a busy bustle of yuppies, though he suspected that term rather dated him. They were hipsters now, weren't they? Or was that term dated and done too? He had no idea.

Bars and cafes were filling up with them whatever they were. The spare trees, barren of their summer foliage, displayed their winter finery; thousands upon thousands of sparkling white lights threaded through their branches and lit the crowds hustling along the sidewalk. It was getting into the Christmas shopping season and the city's cheer showed.

Down the block, the J&M was already packed, one of the liveliest Seattle bars. Two doors down he could already hear the painfully loud rock roaring out from the Central, perhaps the loudest bar in Seattle.

He pulled up the collar on his denim jacket and turned to trudge up the hill back to Pike Street. He could practically hear Richie moaning at him in sympathy, "Aw, Hogan man."

Hogan had to fix this; it was beyond embarrassing.

He hit a cash machine and pulled out a twenty-dollar bill. He timed his arrival at Maria's window to be after the initial morning regulars, but before she'd have run down her supplies. He'd given himself a stern talking to, so he was as ready as he could be.

Except when he arrived at the window Maria wasn't there. A younger, slender Italian beauty sat there instead. He stumbled to a halt, uncertain what to do now.

The young woman spotted him and waved him over.

He staggered forward the few steps out of the chill rain and into the basking warmth of the overhead heater, dry beneath the cheery red-and-white awning.

"You must be the one Maria described. Manuel," she called back over her shoulder to someone deeper inside the kitchen, "he's here." She handed him coffee, but not the trademark *cornetto*.

"Where's…" The woman didn't even let him finish the sentence. Which was good, he didn't know if calling her Maria when he didn't actually know her was being too forward.

"She's off with her son Angelo. They're looking at a new place for his second restaurant." Her accent was light, mostly American with just a hint of the sensuous tones that filled Maria's voice.

Angelo. Angelo's Tuscan Hearth Ristorante. Everyone knew, even he knew, about the sensation Angelo was creating with his fine Italian cuisine. He was smashing barriers with his traditional cooking techniques and innovative flavors. So many chefs were trending in the opposite direction until it often didn't even look like food. French gastronomy had become wholly unrecognizable. Angelo had created his art for the palate rather than the eyes.

Maria was Angelo's mother. He'd never met the man, but it was hard to picture her as old enough to have a son grown, never mind one who'd had time to become a rising star at a national, possibly even international level. Oddly, he liked the sound of that. He'd felt a little guilty at his own forty-five to be drawn to a younger woman. It was far too cliché for a Microsoft Millionaire, such a common phrase in Seattle parlance that it had become a title, to be chasing a younger woman. But he and Maria were of an age, which he liked.

"Here you go, *signore*." She held out a to-go container. He almost lost it to the pavement. By the weight of it, there must be a full meal in there, sold out the back window of one of Seattle's finest restaurants. Sold. Right. He fished after the twenty-dollar bill he'd taken care to slip in his front pocket.

"No," the young woman held up a hand, palm out. "She specifically said that your money was no good here."

"But I'm not—"

The woman waved him off again. "Maria was very insistent. And you have no idea what a serious set of circumstances that implies if I ignore it."

He prepared to sally forth once again, but a cluster of locals had arrived and began greeting "Graziella" and making a fuss of asking after Maria. Without even being conscious of it, he was shifted backward until he had departed the warmth of both the window and the heater, was past the protection of the awning, and stood once again on the cold wet brick of Post Alley.

He retreated to a quiet spot, back by the same brick corner he had occupied the day before. He leaned there out of the rain and sniffed the Styrofoam container. It smelled glorious!

He opened it and was pleased to find a small plastic fork had been included. That was a good thing, because it smelled so amazing he would have scooped it up with his bare hands.

An omelet with smoked salmon and another taste that took him a moment to place, it was so unexpected. Fresh artichoke heart and some tangy cheese, mascarpone. His tongue was too unskilled to even begin to unravel the delicate spicing beyond salt, pepper, and a touch of fresh basil. One of Maria's *cornetto* had also been included, a delicate center of the lightest lemon and basil custard, with a glaze of slivered almonds and browned butter. It cried to be eaten first.

Hogan did his best to appreciate each bite, but knew he was practically inhaling it.

He really did have to fix this silly misunderstanding, but he hadn't had such a tasty meal in a long time. He enjoyed it immensely, totally unaware of the cold rain from above, or the woman watching him ever so sadly from the nearby doorway before she entered the restaurant with her son.

CHAPTER 4

Maria had hoped for a few interesting responses to her advertisement. She sat quietly while the shells were baking for tonight's Winter Custard Tart. It would be a dark chocolate custard with slivers of dried pear, apple, and apricot partially reconstituted in a spicy mulled cider. She'd come out to the front of house and was using the computer tucked discreetly into Graziella's greeting station.

The soft warmth of the interior design based on Ligurian countryside villas, and the beautiful photos that Russell had taken while honeymooning there to decorate the walls, made it feel like home. She had lived seventeen years in Italy, thirty in New York, and now six months here in Seattle, but this restaurant was what felt like home. Somehow she still felt more Italian than American.

The lights were low. The gray day shining weakly through the high windows leant a warmth to the dusky yellows and brick-reds of the décor, and the dark wood and the so-dark-red-they-were-almost-black tablecloths.

She looked down at the computer screen and was stunned to discover that she didn't have a few responses. Her ad had elicited dozens upon dozens of responses. Only momentarily overwhelmed, she quickly came up with a plan. She would treat this like any grocery order, sorting the produce into good enough for the customer, possibly acceptable, and for the trash.

Perhaps the restaurant should give some real produce to one of the homeless shelters, they must always be desperate for supplies. Yes, she must speak to Angelo and Manuel about doing just that with any of their castoffs or unsold product. For one of the secrets of Angelo's Tuscan Hearth was that everything used was fresh that day. Only soups or sauces that needed to stand overnight to mellow and blend were exempt.

That would be good, especially if it helped feed people like the nervous man who had come back to the window this morning. No, not nervous. He hadn't seemed nervous when they met in Pioneer Square last night. Nor was it shyness.

He was tentative, she decided. So painfully tentative. As if he had lost all self-confidence and had found no way yet to make up for the loss.

Whereas the men, and they were almost exclusively men, who had answered her ad could use a large lesson in humility. Well, she would do her part on that front. She simply deleted every one who talked about sex. Not that she didn't want that as well, but it was not where you started a relationship. Especially not a friendship.

"I liked your ad, Ms. Parrano."

Maria jolted only slightly as she looked up at Graziella. She had swept quietly into the front of the restaurant and begun preparing it for the day. Checking supplies of napkins, fresh tablecloths, tall pitchers of ice water. Well, she hadn't expected to fool a woman as sharp as Graziella.

"You know that is Maria to you."

She shrugged, "I know, but I like calling you Ms. Parrano. It just feels more fitting."

"It feels old," Maria riposted.

Graziella's laugh lit up the room. "I am younger than your son."

"Don't remind me. You are such a beautiful girl."

"Thank you. I like your ad. It is hard. Men only see us as…" she indicated her body with a wave of her hand.

"And you are complaining?"

"No…" Graziella pulled out the menus and began inserting the day's lunch menu. "But I wish they were interested in more."

Maria smiled to herself. She knew what Graziella meant. Then she saw an opportunity.

"Is there perhaps one person in particular you wished was paying more attention to you?"

Graziella's soft blush and averted eyes were all Maria needed to see. That the girl's eyes had traveled toward the kitchen door before looking down only confirmed what she already knew.

She reached out and with a brush on the cheek drew the girl's attention back to her. "Sometimes my dear girl, it is the woman who must do the acting."

"But what if he—" Then she clapped a hand over her mouth as if she was afraid of what she'd suddenly revealed.

Maria pulled her in and kissed her on each cheek despite the hand still firmly clapped over her mouth.

"You are so sweet. First, if he does not fall down at your feet in praise to the Almighty, he does not appreciate you enough. Second, Maria thinks he will do exactly that. All you must do? Let him know that it is welcome. He is too busy being careful around his boss and forgetting how to be a man."

"But Angelo—"

"Phhtt!" Maria waved a hand as if shooing a fly. "My son, he is very good at not seeing anything, not even what is right in front of his face. Just ask that charming fiancée of his. I will fix him good if he makes any fuss. Now leave this old woman to her e-mail, you have a lunch to be serving."

Graziella's laugh, gorgeous smile, and quick hug left Maria

feeling her age. Not old, but no longer young either. In that middle of life like a good wine, she decided. She would have to remind herself of that when she was with such a young woman.

She turned back to the responses to her ad. Both younger men and older soon traced the "sex talkers" path into her trash. Why a nineteen-year-old was seeking a "hot mama" was not a question she was the least interested in answering. Nor why men in their seventies thought they could possibly keep up with her.

She wanted to do so much. She had never been drawn to the outdoors, but that didn't mean she didn't want to try it. Maria wanted to learn, explore, and be shocked in wonder. She knew what she'd wanted ever since she'd first heard the phrase, "to suck the marrow from life." Like a good Osso Buco, braised veal shanks over risotto, she'd craved that feeling.

Then she reached an e-mail that brought her to a screeching halt.

The Terrific Trio requests the company of
Maria Amelia Avico Parrano.
Tonight, Cutter's Crabhouse, 6 pm.

No sender's name. Nothing about who the "Terrific Trio" might be. And not a hint of how they knew not only that it was her advertisement, but knew her full name as well.

She deleted it. All those responses, and not a one had made it into her "possibly acceptable" list. She closed her e-mail.

And felt nothing but sadness.

That was not her normal state. The instant she stood and looked about the quiet restaurant, awaiting the start of yet another lunch service, she knew exactly where she would be at six o'clock this evening.

Maria had vacillated and worried. Her plans to leave the restaurant early enough to go home and change were sabotaged by a lunch rush that used up too many dark-chocolate-dipped, cherry biscotti and she had to make more for dinner to go with her fresh-made hazelnut gelato served in an almond-brandy snap cup.

She did consider going to Perrin's Glorious Garb. Her boy was marrying Jo, a lovely lawyer of Alaskan heritage who had recently taken over as the manager of the Pike Place Market. One of her friends was an amazing clothier named Perrin Williams. Another of her friends had married dear Russell.

Cassidy Knowles also appeared to be the first woman other than herself who had made any success of controlling Russell's restless energy. Maria had channeled Russell and Angelo's energy by teaching them to cook. Cassidy and Jo apparently both applied a liberal dose of common sense, they kept the two men so in love with them that they never knew which way their heads were spinning.

She had left the new lovebirds alone as much as possible. Jo and Angelo were all young and didn't need her hanging about them. She'd shopped at Perrin's store a few times. While the clothes were so beautiful, they made the clothes the statement. Maria preferred to wear clothes that attracted attention, but let her be the statement.

So, she went through the Market on the way to Cutter's, leaving herself enough time to browse the shops and stalls.

She found a Christmas scarf that completely suited her ideas of taste. It wasn't candy canes and red-cheeked Santas. It was an abstract wash of holly and candle flames. As if it were made for La Festa di Santa Lucia. While that wasn't for almost two weeks, Maria liked the way it brought out the red in her dark hair. It made her feel very festive, which is how a woman should feel around the holidays.

She'd planned on arriving early. That way she could be

sipping a glass of wine when the self-proclaimed "Terrific Trio" arrived. She was betting with herself that it was Joseph, Clara, and William. They were so often there right when she opened her window. And, she was pleased to note, they had the good sense to bring their ever-rotating line of dates to Angelo's for a proper meal when they wanted to impress them. They were fun and pleasant, it would be a nice evening, that she'd be unlikely to repeat.

If it was someone else, well then, she'd just wait and see. She wasn't above pretending her phone buzzed from the restaurant with a "dessert emergency." She'd have to remember that one, it was a funny line.

Maria was actually a little late by the time she arrived, the scarf had been in one of the last places she'd looked. The invitation hadn't said whether they were to meet in the bar or the restaurant.

The restaurant was down a long corridor, passing through the servers' prep station. It would have been strange if not for the spectacular view that lay in wait for the unsuspecting patron.

The bar sprawled to the left as she entered the door. It was filled with the young and the professionals. So much so that she almost felt out of place. Lawyers radiated power with their suits, but most others dressed to be seen. Even the scruffy, and several of the people had that upscale scruffy look that only comes with success in some software business or the like, were young and exceedingly healthy.

Well, Maria Amelia, you can turn tail and run, or you can fling your power scarf over your shoulder and sweep into the room as if you are the one who belongs.

She did the latter and swept in. It was pleasing to see several men turn to watch her passage toward the long wooden bar at the far end of the lounge, despite their dates' glares. In front of the bar stood a line of stools, mostly occupied, but with none of the dedicated drinkers typical in most bars. No, people came here to see and be seen, not to be life-long patrons.

Opposite the bar was a long wall of glass looking south along the Seattle waterfront. Six o'clock was well past dark on a December night and the city glowed. Pike Place Market was a blare of light to the left.

The view seemed to tumble down the high cliff of Western and into the water past the brightly lit piers of restaurants, tourist shops, and the ferry terminal. Beyond the big new Ferris wheel the view went dark, the expanse of Elliot Bay only lit by the occasional ferry across the water looking like a birthday cake bearing far too many candles. The mountain backdrop had disappeared with the darkness, just the faintest orange outline showing the towering snowy mountains.

The view fit Cutter's Bar, filling it with the vibrancy of what was actually quite a quaint city. They were so proud of all their industry and busy doings, the largest city in the Northwest, the portal to Alaska, the bicycling capital of the U. S... Their lists went on and on.

She had lived thirty years in New York, the city that never slept. Most of Seattle would be closed by eight o'clock. It was young and terribly pleased with itself, like so many of the patrons she could see in the bar.

"Maria, over here."

She turned, and stumbled to a halt. All of her self-contained bravado slipping off her shoulders like a lost shawl at the surprise. She didn't know if she was ready to face *this* trio. They had seen the ad and knew her secret loneliness.

At one of the small round window tables, tall with equally high stools that put them on display, sat three beautiful young women.

Cassidy Knowles in her trademark black turtleneck, designer slacks, and leather, calf-length boots. To either side, Jo Thompson ever so formal in her charcoal lawyer power suit, and Perrin in, well, full-on Perrin was probably the only way to describe her.

The woman's shoulder-length hair was white. Not white-blonde, but white. Her dress and leggings beneath were black and form-fitting, even black gloves revealing only her fingertips with unpainted nails. It was as if only her hair and face existed and the rest of her was invisible.

It should have looked alien, as if she'd fallen out of a science-fiction movie. Or perhaps Goth. Instead, Maria could see, it was making even the male waiters stumble as they passed by. She was far and away the most stunning woman in the room tonight.

Maria sidled up to the table. She actually always felt daunted by her daughter-in-law-to-be and her two friends. They were a family and she wasn't. They traced their lineage all the way back to their first day at college. Maria had never graduated from upper secondary, leaving at seventeen, a year early due to her pregnancy. They were so terribly accomplished; all Maria had ever done was give birth to a son and cook.

"You are the Terrific Trio?" In a way they were. They quite unnerved her.

"Guilty," Perrin declared brightly.

"And proud to be," Russell's wife, Cassidy offered.

"No," Angelo's Jo stopped them all with her calm composure and simple declarative.

"No?" the others asked.

"There are four of us now."

"The Fab Four?" Cassidy offered.

"I've got it," Perrin raised her glass in a black-gloved hand for a toast.

There was a brief delay while they found a drink for Maria to toast with. She took the moment to climb onto the stool that placed them nearly elbow to elbow around the table, though it left her feeling as if she were teetering.

"We are hereby the Fearsome Foursome."

"Hear. Hear." The others raised their glasses, so Maria followed suit.

Perrin knocked back the rest of her Cosmopolitan.

Jo and Cassidy sipped their wine.

Maria knocked back the sip of Perrin's Cosmo that had been poured into an empty water glass for her.

She and Perrin slammed their glasses back down on the table and said in unison, "Hear. Hear."

And just that fast, they welcomed Maria into their inner circle. Suddenly she was very glad she'd come.

"BUT HOW DO you know it was me?" Maria sipped at her wine. Cassidy had picked a local white that perfectly complemented the Oven Roasted Dungeness and Rock Crab Dip. The dish was good, not subtle, but good. The wine pairing definitely elevated it.

"Only someone as dense as my Angelo could miss that," Jo shook her head sadly. Her long, straight black hair swirled across her shoulders: the only indicator of her Alaskan heritage other than her perfect dusky skin. That she was such a beauty and had just been ranked as one of Seattle's most influential women only made Maria wonder how her son, who she loved dearly, had been good enough.

"Go Angelo," was all she could think.

"Russell is dense enough. He's even worse than Angelo," Cassidy offered with a thoroughly contented sigh.

"Yes, or Russell," Jo conceded. "Only two such men wouldn't know it was you, Maria. The instant Angelo showed me the newspaper, I knew…and I felt awful."

"Why awful?"

"You were so kind to me when Angelo and I were stumbling

our way toward each other, then… I shall be kind to myself by just saying, then I dropped you."

Maria reached out and held Jo's hand. "You, my dear girl, are in a terribly demanding new job and newly in love. The last thing you need to be worrying about is foolish old mother-in-law."

Jo's strong hand squeezed back.

"The next time you say that you're old, you'll be wearing a Cosmo," Perrin raised her glass in threat.

"But I am."

"Before you came, we all agreed, you are the woman we want to grow up to be. We've also decided that you are our style guru. If you weren't so totally scary, we'd have thought to do this much sooner."

"Scary? Me?" There was an adjective she'd never have picked in a thousand years.

"You're beautiful."

"You cook like a dream."

"You dress in a way that just pisses me off." Perrin declared with a shake of her white-white hair. "You always look so effortless. Me, I'm…constructed." She waved to indicate her styling and clothes.

"But that is you, my dear," Maria protested. "You are so much breathtaking that I know half the men in the room must be needing neck braces before the night is over."

"Really?" Perrin appeared surprised. As if she didn't know or trust her own startling beauty. She glanced over Maria's shoulder cautiously.

"They will all have sore necks from turning so often to admire you. And many will go home wearing their date's drinks in their face for staring so often. That I promise." That one of these women could be less than confident shocked her to the very core.

"You know what makes you really scary?" Cassidy's soft

voice stopped the back-and-forth flow of conversation around the table.

Maria shook her head. Realized she was crumpling her napkin in her lap with her nerves and forced herself to stop even if she couldn't relax.

It was Jo who answered. "How in the world did you raise Russell and Angelo without having to murder at least one of them? That is the true miracle."

"Oh, that was easy," she laughed at their aghast expressions. "Best way to a young boy's head is through his stomach. And when they start noticing girls? I started feeding the girls as well. I make it so the boys never thought twice about bringing them to my kitchen. Then Maria would quietly scoot the worst ones right back out the door without the boys even noticing."

"Scary smart," Jo confirmed.

"Totally," Cassidy freshened their wine glasses.

"Wish you'd been my mother," Perrin's voice was soft, barely loud enough for Maria to hear. The look on her face wasn't silly or joking as it had been until this moment. It was very real and remarkably sad.

Maria felt herself melt. Without even thinking, she took Perrin's hand, pulled her into a leaning hug, and kissed her atop her shining hair. They sat back up, but Perrin stared down at the white tablecloth.

Maria knew that lack of a mother had been one of the common bonds between these three friends. Cassidy's had died young, Jo's had abandoned her family while Jo was still a toddler, and Perrin's mother had been abusive in some fashion meaning that she didn't deserve the title. Maria had to wipe her eyes at the pain she saw on Perrin's features.

"I could wish that too, dear," she whispered to Perrin. "You are wonderful woman and anyone who didn't see that... Well, they did no deserve you."

Perrin looked up at her, staring until she could see that

Maria meant it, tears began trickling down her cheeks and Maria wiped them away fighting against her own.

"Hey," Cassidy protested. "What did we just miss? No crying at this table unless we all do. That's the rule."

Maria kept Perrin's hand in her own as she faced the others. She looked at each of these amazing women.

"I loved raising such boys. But I always dreamed of daughters. I just never dreamed of daughters like you three."

"Oh man." Cassidy groaned.

Jo blinked hard then actually sniffled in a terribly un-Jo-like fashion. "Okay, that did it. You are hereafter stuck with us forever."

Perrin looked away, studying the table in silence. But she didn't release her tight hold on Maria's hand.

It had taken a fresh round of appetizers and drinks to clear the mood of the table.

Taylor Shellfish Farms Steamed Manila Clams saw them through several "Russell and Angelo as young boys" stories.

A fresh basket of Cutter's trademark focaccia, practically dripping with olive oil and garlic, covered the latest updates on Perrin's love life. She was desperately in and out of love at least once a month. Her heart apparently only had two modes, full-on and full-off.

Maria privately concluded that her own heart had perhaps been set to full-off without her realizing it. Yes, it was time to change that as well.

When Cassidy ordered another bottle of wine, this time a magnificent Willamette Valley Pinot Blanc, Maria began to worry about quite how much everyone was drinking, including herself.

"Oh no, not to worry," Perrin signaled the waiter for a fresh Cosmo. "It's another rule of the Terrific Trio."

"Fearsome Foursome," Cassidy corrected her absently as she inspected the new wine as only one of the nation's leading food-and-wine critics could.

"Fabulous Fivesome if one of you in married types would please, please, please go ahead and get pregnant so I could be an auntie." Perrin was on a roll. And when she was, there was clearly no stopping her.

Jo's voice practically squeaked, shattering her eternally calm outer demeanor. "Not even married yet."

Cassidy blanched white at the thought and raised her hands in surrender.

"See?" Perrin turned to Maria. "Stingy, that's what they are. Anyway, the rule is, we're not allowed to get drunk unless we're all together. Ever since college we've had that rule."

"And we've paid for it," Jo's tone was drily funny, suggesting wild escapades.

Maria would guess that those wild times were Perrin's doing. As a matter of fact, she would bet on it. And something about Jo's eyes and a shared glance with Cassidy. Yes, they had made the rule to protect Perrin from herself.

Perrin must not know that about her friends, for she took a totally different reading from Jo's sidelong glance and poked a finger in Cassidy's arm.

"Of course one of us, and I *am* pointing fingers…" In fact, she was forcing Cassidy to lean sideways towards Jo to escape the pressure. "…broke that rule and got horribly smashed in private."

"Those were unusual circumstances, Perrin." Jo spoke in Cassidy's defense even as she batted away Perrin's hand and helped Cassidy back upright.

"Yeah," Perrin's gaze returned to Maria. She leaned in confidentially and rested her chin on her fist even though her elbow was nowhere near the table, as if she was so ethereal that she could rest in mid-air.

"Such unusual circumstances that Russell had to break down her condo door with his shoulder." Perrin winked and rolled her eyes back toward Cassidy before reaching once more for her drink.

Cassidy and Jo might think they had Perrin bamboozled, but Maria wondered if it might not be the other way around. Perrin knew exactly why the "only get drunk together" rule existed, even if she cooperated with it for the sake of self-preservation, but she wasn't above getting vengeance on Cassidy for underestimating her.

Well, as two could play at that game, she winked back at Perrin before turning to Cassidy.

"So," Maria took a careful sip of her wine and reached for another piece of focaccia. "After Russell breaks down the door and you are all drunkenness by yourself, did he make you naked?"

Perrin almost snorted her Cosmo.

CHAPTER 5

Maria decided she was awake, what she couldn't decide was if it was safe to be. She eyed the alarm clock accusingly, but it hadn't gone off. Not for three more minutes.

She turned it off and sat up tentatively but with only a little twinge. Perhaps, as Cassidy claimed, hangovers were lessened by good vintages and exceptional friends. For whatever reason, other than a small headache that a few aspirin would easily cure, she felt surprisingly good. In some ways she felt better than she had in a long time.

They been such...fun!

Russell's mother, Julia Morgan, despite how close they'd been, had been her employer. Julia was the billionaire's wife; Maria was her personal chef. She'd had woman friends, but they had appeared only on occasion and drifted away just as readily. Maria's entire life had been the Morgan family and raising the boys.

Last night had been a surprise in more ways than one. It hadn't just been a discovery of friends, it had also been a discovery of self. Of how much she'd enjoyed being with other women. Once over the initial surprise, the Terrific Trio had settled in and treated her no differently than they did one another. No layers of respect or distance.

Perrin had dubbed her Mama Maria and Cassidy had jumped right on board with the nickname. Only Jo, ever so reserved Jo, had called her simply Maria. And it hadn't added distance, instead it had somehow been closer, as if she truly had gained a daughter-in-law.

The girls had debated, at embarrassing length, about who to set Maria up with. Perrin had offered several actors, a rock-and-roll guitarist, two different lawyers she'd become bored with, and might well have kept going if Maria hadn't diverted the conversation to who was going to someday capture Perrin's heart.

Maria had now daydreamed past her normal rising time and the baking awaited. Angelo's Pioneer Square condo had little personality, little to hold her here other than a magnificent kitchen that there was little time to use.

When she first moved to Seattle, she'd considered fixing it up, imagining how she and Angelo would design it together. Place a large table in the middle of the dining room and always have it surrounded by friends and laughter and good food.

Then Angelo had moved into Jo's gorgeous high-rise.

He, in typical Angelo fashion, had decorated nothing other than the kitchen. The rest of the rooms were clearly the result of a single run to IKEA. The darkly rich hardwood floor had a few scattered rugs. There were some cheery posters on the walls, but no art and little family.

It didn't feel neglected, it was far too nice a condominium for that. It was comfortable, but it didn't feel like home either. Fixing it up didn't seem important, not when it was just herself. As if it was temporary even though she had no reason to think it was.

There was so little to hold her here. So, she showered, chose a soft-wool red dress and a matching coat that always made her feel as if she were wrapped in a winter fire's warmth, and headed out.

Pioneer Square was still dark and quiet on the cold December morning. Unusually, the sky was clear and she could see the brighter stars and a quarter moon despite the streetlights. A couple of very early risers were shuffling out of the Lawrence Shelter, grabbing a quick smoke huddled together on the sidewalk while waiting for breakfast. She could already smell the characteristic notes on the still air of warming griddles and hot coffee. She hoped the man was still tucked in somewhere warm, she liked picturing the stranger that way.

First Avenue showed only a little of its reputedly seedy past, especially at this hour. The streets were quiet except for the occasional bus. She knew from experience, these were the very first runs of the day. Some mornings she'd step aboard rather than make the eight-block, uphill trek, but today she chose to enjoy the walk. It would also help her work off some of the splendid excesses of last night.

The sidewalk trees were lit with white Christmas lights strung through their branches making them appear coated in crystalline sugar. Shop windows had acquired buntings and garlands. Magic Mouse Toys was, of course, a child's dream of quirky toys. It wasn't New York's mad display at FAO Schwartz at a tenth the size, but it had a sweetness that the other lacked. The gray stone building and its brightly lit windows invited you in, even though the interior would be dark for hours yet.

A coffee shop, not yet open, had filled their window with an entire Santa's village landscape of miniatures, ranging across imaginary coffee-cup icebergs, down bagged-coffee hills.

She enjoyed her walk, a refreshing stroll. The three women, her three self-declared and sworn-for-life daughters, had given her much to think about last night.

There was a change coming.

She didn't know what it might be, but could feel it as surely as a sauce finally coming together. Maria felt that her life, like her cooking, was perhaps best if she let it run intuitively, so she would let it this time as well.

For thirty years her life had been about the stability of the Morgan household. Six months ago with her move to Seattle, it had become about Angelo's restaurant and his courtship of Jo. Maybe this time it would be about her.

She decided that her new friends would approve. If Maria saw change for herself coming, well, she'd welcome it.

Hogan loved the city in the morning, before it was filled with people and crowds. Vera had been a night owl, but he was a morning person, often going for long walks while she still slept. Merely one of the thousand complaints she'd leveled at him.

He had leveled only one at her, infidelity. He only discovered in court the vast extent of her attempts to belittle his manhood, never mind their marriage. The worst part was that it had worked. His lawyer had made sure that she walked away without a single dime of his Microsoft money, and he'd crawled into his condo and disappeared.

Well, he was sick of that. It was time for him to climb back out of his hole. And he knew right where he was going to start. The next time he saw Maria, he'd straighten out all this nonsense of his being homeless and destitute. He might be a lost cause, but he didn't need charity. Not like so many he'd seen. He just needed—

A vision riveted Hogan to the sidewalk by the flower stall at the top of the Market. It was as if his feet had been glued to the brickwork. A woman was walking toward him. She was a vision of fire in the dark, a flame-wrapped wonder with a shock of dark hair that caught red from the streetlights and offered it up as a beacon in the night.

Maria. Before he could react, she had turned down the sidewalk into the Market, a turn that led her away from where he still stood in the shadows.

There would be no better chance than the present. Before he could think of a hundred reasons not to, he called out her name. She turned, and then her face lit with a smile of recognition.

She stopped and waited beneath the bright triple-globe of the antique streetlight that highlighted her like a shop-window ornament.

It took consciously forcing his knees to bend, but he did get his feet moving.

"Good morning, Maria." It didn't come out as too much of a croak, more as if he simply hadn't used his voice yet today. Didn't it?

"Good morning. You know, I do not even know how to be calling you."

"Hogan," *Dummy would be bloody appropriate as well.* "Hogan Stanford."

"A pleasure, Hogan Stanford." She held out a gloved hand which he shook after too long a hesitation.

He had lost all social graces.

"You couldn't have eaten before leaving the shelter. Are their breakfasts not any good?"

"I, uh, wouldn't know," he only volunteered afternoons to help with the dinner service.

"Then where do you normally eat?"

He almost turned and pointed up at his condo window. It hung a dozen stories above them and a block to the side. But that felt stupid as if he were too clumsy to speak or explain. He started to form a sentence in his mind.

"You don't. Well, come with me. We take care of that." She

slipped her hand about his elbow and began to lead him into the Market.

"No, wait, you don't even know me. I could be—" What, a crazed psycho? Even in her most vile epithets, Vera hadn't accused him of that. Hogan Q. Milquetoast had been her nickname for him in the courtroom, which had won her little ground with the judge.

Maria stopped and smiled up at him, as if she knew more about him that he did.

"I'm not poor," he finally blurted out.

"Of course not," Maria agreed amiably. "There are always people worse off than we are. That is kind of you, Hogan Stanford." She made to lead him off again.

The fishmonger, the one always loudly professing his undying love, began opening his shop. Just an easy shout away. He began relaxing on Maria's behalf, not that she needed protection from him.

This was all getting too muddled.

"Maria," he dug in his heels to keep them in place until this was settled.

She turned to face him once again with absolute patience, as if she were dealing with the feeble-minded. Her face wasn't angelic. It was far too filled with life to be so described. It was rich with laugh lines, full lips, and the most expressive eyes on the planet. Sophia Loren could envy such eyes.

"I don't eat at the shelter because I volunteer there. I help out, I don't want to take their food."

"And you dress…"

He looked down and reassessed his clothes from an outsider's perspective. She'd judged him as broke because his clothes were old and worn. That wasn't it at all. He shrugged, "I dress…comfortably."

Maria covered her mouth with two gloved fingers of her

free hand. In moments, he could see the look of consternation turning into a smile.

He smiled in response.

"Well, that is one on me, is it not?" Her hand remained wrapped in the crook of his elbow. "Well, Mr. Stanford, I say that I make you breakfast, and I make you breakfast. Come along."

Her gentle tug got him in motion.

"And while I am cooking, you can explain how a man who is not poor, came to be at my window with no money."

Great. Once he explained that he'd only had hundred-dollar bills in his pocket, she'd probably think he was a drug-runner. No, they probably dressed better than he did.

MARIA WAS FIRST into the restaurant. She had always enjoyed this part of the day. The front of the house dark except for a few small sconce lights left on for safety. The kitchen lit only over her workspace, the rest of it filled with soft shadows and the fading reminders of last night's good smells.

She placed Hogan on a nearby stool and started a small pot of coffee.

"Can I help?"

"No, you are my guest. You may sit and tell me about yourself while I recover from my deep embarrassment."

"You don't look embarrassed, you look radiant."

She glanced up in time to see him blush. She was past blushing, but she wasn't past being flattered. She allowed him a moment to recover as she sliced day-old baguette and put it in the toaster. A nice, ripe Roma tomato slice, paper-thin bits of prosciutto, a dusting of minced basil, and a drizzle of olive oil on the toast. It was all ready just as the coffee finished brewing.

He still hadn't spoken, but it hadn't been an uncomfortable silence. She'd rather enjoyed having him watch her cook.

Radiant? That was a good word, she liked that one.

She set the breakfast between them on a single plate, and two large mugs of coffee. That was one of the American innovations that she liked, the ridiculously oversized coffee mug. What they lacked was any idea of what coffee should taste like. Even Seattle, so famous for its roasts, was typically lacking.

"Wow! That will wake you up," Hogan was staring down into his coffee mug as if it had just attacked him.

"What, you like weak American coffee?"

"No," he ignored her teasing tone. "But I do think that it's a good thing I'm not planning to try and sleep again this week. Have you seen my eyebrows anywhere? I think your coffee knocked them off my forehead." He began inspecting the kitchen floor as if he were indeed searching for them.

She pointed above his eyes.

He reached up and tested that they were still there before releasing a huge sigh of relief.

Maria felt the lifting of her spirits, but masked them with a bite of bruschetta.

He joined her. "Wow, that's perfect. 'The perfect bite' as they say on the cooking shows. But this can't be all you eat."

This time she actually laughed. "This is more than I usually eat. I make this for my guest. Italian breakfast is a biscuit or *cornetto* and strong coffee. It is enough."

"So, your morning window service, that is more properly Italian?"

"If they are plain or filled with a little honey or marmalade, yes. As I make them for Americans?" she shrugged.

HOGAN WAS FINDING Maria to be amazingly easy to talk with. Casual conversation had always been one of his weakest skills. He could lead a programming team of a hundred individuals and a half-dozen supervisors. What he couldn't do was meet them in the bar after work and not be stilted.

"I arrived at Microsoft just as they were launching their first really stable Windows platform. That was version 3.0a, back in 1989. Summer intern, hotshot geek straight out of the University of Washington."

"You are local boy?"

"Yep. Born and raised." He became fascinated with watching her move about the kitchen. It wasn't that she was so beautiful. Okay, it wasn't only that. He liked to think he was above merely prurient fantasies, though Maria's body could convince him otherwise. But he did enjoy watching how she cooked aside from that. There was a confidence, an assuredness as she mixed flour, yeast, butter, and a half-dozen other ingredients. No recipe, no second guessing, rarely any measuring cups.

"True locals are rare according to Angelo." Her voice was as rich as her coffee was strong. He liked food metaphors for her, they seemed to fit naturally.

He shook off the fascination with what she was doing and refocused on the conversation. "We are. I always say that Seattle is forty percent California refugees, forty percent East Coast refugees, ten percent from the Midwest, though no one knows why, and ten percent natives, but we're hiding."

Her laugh was musical. It lit the darkened kitchen far more than the spotlight dangling over her station. He scratched his head and wondered how on earth he could possibly make her laugh again. It was a sound he could never tire of hearing.

"And you are in hiding? From what?"

That stopped him. Yes, he certainly was in hiding, but how to explain the darkness inside him to this brilliantly shining woman who stood before him. She'd have no way to understand something so polar opposite to who she was.

"Myself mostly." Far too close to the truth. Couldn't he have just said "Californians" or "lawyers" or "hipsters" or anything else funny? No, he never thought up the punch line until two beats too late. The first beat, when it would have been funny if he'd said it then. The second beat, right after he'd said something far too true.

Back in his old life someone might say, "The system crashes every time I run your code."

He couldn't think to reply, "Have you tried walking it instead?" No, he had to stammer and apologize and promise to work harder. Though he'd become a hell of a good programmer just so he could stop apologizing for his hard work.

"Who was she?" Maria took the dough she'd been preparing and put it in a big standup refrigerator, pulling out another large batch she must have started yesterday.

"My wife."

He saw a brief flash of disappointment across Maria's features. So fleeting that he wondered if even she was aware of it.

"My ex-wife," he corrected.

"And she hurt you so badly?"

What was it with this conversation? Not only was he several steps too exposed, he couldn't catch up with it at all.

"She…" How to describe the impact her vast betrayal had had upon him. Who was he kidding, that it still had upon him.

No. He couldn't face the next sentence. It was too hard.

"Perhaps I should leave you to your cooking. Thank you for—"

Maria aimed a slender rolling pin at his chest across the table.

"No. You can no leave yet. You have not finished your breakfast."

He looked down. There were still several bruschetta on the plate and his coffee was barely half empty. "If I drink any more of your coffee, I'll need an FAA license for flying through restricted airspace."

Her gentle smile was no less potent than her laugh. "Well," Maria attacked the dough with a dusting of flour and a great deal of energy. "In trouble with the FAA would not be good kind of trouble. Maybe you need lessons to flying under the radar."

"Nowhere low enough to escape Vera's radar." Even to himself he sounded pissed and bitter.

Maria stopped rolling out the dough and studied him for a long moment. Her dark eyes were shadowed by the overhead light. He could feel himself spread as thin as the dough with all his faults clearly visible. Here was where she decided he was too screwed up to bother dealing with and she'd send him on his way.

"There is now a new rule."

"There is?"

"There is," she nodded emphatically to herself. "Yes, it is a good rule. Until I tell you otherwise, Mr. Hogan Stanford, you are no allowed to say that name again or talk about her. Not one word. Not even to yourself if you can help it."

All he could do was stare at her. "You're serious?"

"You doubt that, you ask my son. Do not mess with Mama Maria. *Proibito!* You will not talk about her, refer to her, what is the word I want, *alludere?*"

"Allude?"

"That simple? Yes, you will not even do that. Not until I decide you are cured of whatever cloud she make over your head."

"She—"

Maria cut him off with a sharp gesture of a single finger to her lips. "I will stop you every time you mention her. Who else do you talk to about her? You must tell them also to stop you."

"Uh, I don't talk to anyone else."

She turned back to her dough, setting a dinner plate rim-down on the dough. With a quick trace of her knife around the edge, she cut a circle. Lifting the plate, she sliced a dozen lines through the dough with the tip of a sharp knife creating long thin triangles that all met at the center.

"No one else?" She didn't look up from her task. It was as if she was giving him a safe space to speak from.

"Not really." He sipped his coffee.

She plopped spoonfuls of a light-yellow custard at the wide ends of the triangles. She rolled them up one by one and the *cornetti* came into being. Placing them on a baking tray, she shaped them as crescents with a practiced flick. In moments they were lined up, smeared with butter, and adorned with slivered almonds and lemon zest. He could hardly wait to try one. Unbaked, they already looked beautiful.

She maintained her silence until she had completed several trays and slid them into the large ovens ranging along the wall. With a quick swipe, she cleaned off the prep table, then sat on the stool across from him. Taking a bruschetta and her coffee, she finally looked up at him.

It wasn't a look he'd expected. There was no judgment, that he was too much of a loner or what was wrong with him that he didn't have any friends. It was a look of sorrow.

"I talk to everybody." Then she studied the darkness above the worktable lights for a long time before facing him again.

There was just the two of them and the single light. They both sat in the shadows on opposite sides of the table. Mostly what was visible was her hands and her white porcelain cup shining beneath the light.

"But other than three young woman, I think I too may be as alone."

Hogan couldn't imagine how that could be possible, but he didn't question it either. She was clearly a thoughtful woman. She had noticed what he had not, that he had let his life be defined by his past.

"I'm going to return the favor," he raised his coffee mug as if proposing a toast.

"What favor is that?" Though she raised her mug to share the toast.

"I will agree to not speak about, well, you know who. And you will agree to call on me any time you need someone to really talk to. It doesn't have to be about anything, and it can be at three in the morning."

"A new friend?"

He shrugged, "We all have to start somewhere."

After a long moment, that smile lit her face. Really lit it, her eyes shining from the shadows.

"Have to start somewhere? But where does that mean you are heading?"

Huh! He didn't have an answer to that one. He was still surprised that for the first time in a long time, he was really looking forward to spending time with someone.

"I guess we'll have to find that out along the way."

CHAPTER 6

Hogan's door buzzer snapped him out of his morose contemplation of the terrible programming on television for the night.

He'd been at a loss all day.

His attempts to follow Maria's directive not to think about Vera only seemed to have thrown his past into the forefront of his mind. By now it was making him totally crazy. At least he hadn't scorched the chowder pot at the shelter again. Of course, they were having minestrone tonight which didn't burn unless you did something too stupid for even his present state of mind.

He opened the door and almost fell back in shock. There stood Maria Parrano, lovely in a dark blue dress and the same red woolen coat as this morning. Muted with the contrasting blue, she appeared mysterious rather than as a flame under this morning's streetlight. Mysterious was certainly appropriate, as it was a complete mystery as to why she was tolerating him, never mind seeking him out.

"May I come in?" Her voice teased him for his gawking and fumbling, but did it with a kindness.

"Of course." It was only as she entered, that he noticed the two flattened moving boxes under one arm.

"What are those for?"

"Hogan Stanford," she stopped and looked up at him. "There are several things you need to learn for us to be becoming friends. The first is to greet me, the second is to be a gentleman and then to be offering to take my coat."

He fumbled his way through that. She set aside the boxes without explanation.

"Do I get a tour? Or do we remain standing in your entry hall?"

He slapped his forehead with a loud smack. *Get your act together, Stanford.* He took a deep breath to calm himself and then offered her his arm. She took it lightly as he led her in.

THE SHORT HALL opened onto a living room that took Maria's breath away. It wasn't the furnishing, which was nice enough, if a little sparse. It was the view.

Hogan's home was far lower than Jo and Angelo's condominium with its magnificent view from high above Seattle. Hogan's view was no less stunning, but it was also intimate in its closeness to the scenery. The ice-capped Olympic Mountains towered in the dark orange of the evening sky. Elliot Bay was spread before them as not even Cutter's Bar had shown it off last night. And, as they came up to the glass, she could see Pike Place Market spread at her feet. It made the world look like it was the inside of a jewel box.

"Why Hogan, this is *fantastico.*"

"Uh, thanks. Why are you here?"

She could hear that he hadn't intended it to sound offensive. Maria considered teasing him about it, but decided that a man so unaware of *how* he was communicating perhaps cared very much about *what* he was communicating. So, rather than skewering him like a kebab, she answered his question honestly.

"I am here for helping. You can fetch those two boxes while I more admire the view?"

He moved to comply and she turned to inspect the room. The living room had a soft brown leather sofa and matching chair that looked well lived in. That would be his preferred spot. They faced the view more than the television, which she would take as a good sign.

There was a neatness that was surprising for a man so casual about his attire.

The low coffee table sported only the television remotes, a book, and a couple of magazines, *Wired* and *Cook's Illustrated*. Leave it to a computer guy to enjoy the terribly quantitative approach to cooking. She herself had few written recipes, primarily following her instincts and her taste buds.

Another amusing observation that she'd keep to herself were those two magazines. The first was heavily thumbed, a dozen different pages with the corners folded down; clearly topics Hogan wanted to think about and consider more at a later time. *Cook's* was almost pristine. A small crease indicated that it had probably been read, but it didn't inspire.

Beyond the sofa, a long oak table and formal chairs defined a dining space, but looked not just unused, but wholly uninhabited. It should be crowded with friends and family. A jovial gathering place for coming together each week and remembering life's joys in the company of others.

Well, it was not her place to suggest such things in another's life, but if she lived here, it would look as well used as Hogan's chair, not like a museum piece.

The space itself was interesting: the view to the front, a long wall of books to the side, a somewhat barren wall backed the dining table, that should be covered with photos of friends and adventures, but perhaps he didn't have any to hang. The doors along the other side wall must lead to kitchen and bedroom.

Hogan returned with the boxes, and Maria fished a roll of packing tape out of her purse. In moments they were assembled.

He was clearly restraining his questions. Perhaps he had learned that she would only answer them as she saw fit. It meant he was smart about people, whether he communicated that graciously or not.

"Now, my friend Mr. Stanford. You are going to go through your apartment. Everything that was a gift from, or reminds you in any bad way about the woman, who you still aren't allowed to speak of, you will hand to me, and I pack it away."

"Then what?"

"Then we will put these boxes into storage somewhere. Later you may decide if you ever want to open them again. I am hoping that you have enough good sense that two boxes will be sufficient. If you have held onto too much of the woman's past, we can be getting more boxes. You can also be simply throwing things away." She went back to the coat rack by the front door and retrieved a couple of black plastic garbage bags from her coat pocket. "You do not even have to touch anything. You may simply point and tell me to box or to bag."

Then she began to wonder again about the magazines. She walked over and picked up the issue of *Cook's Illustrated*. Maria held it up as a question.

HOGAN STOOD FROZEN, riveted in place in his own living room by the steady gaze of a woman half-a-head shorter than he was. How had she known? He was interested in cooking, enjoyed the editor's opening story and the science behind what they did.

It hadn't been Vera's magazine, but rather one she kept

gifting him year in and year out even though he never cooked anything from it. Yet another little guilt trip he hadn't recognized? Perhaps.

Then he eyed the woman holding the magazine for his decision.

His first instinct was that Maria was trying to be controlling, as Vera had been. Then he winced, knowing he wasn't supposed to be thinking of her, an almost impossible mandate. Contradictory. How do you stop thinking about someone you've been told specifically to be aware of every time you thought about her? A tautological conundrum at best, at worst...bloody impossible.

It was also a depressing shock quite how easily Vera entered his thoughts though the last of the divorce-related tasks was over six months past.

Knowing his first instincts were not to be trusted in anything to do with Vera, he decided that there were two other primary possibilities as to what Maria was up to. First, Maria could be trying to clear any Vera remnants out of his condo to make way for herself. Since she'd thought he was a bum until this morning and he'd not told her how well off he truly was, he considered that as unlikely. Second, maybe he should take her statement at face value. Perhaps she was simply that kind.

A feeling ran through him that he was having trouble identifying. A part of him wanted to wrap his arms around Maria and simply weep.

She didn't wait for him to respond. Reading his expression, she tossed it into the garbage bag. He'd have to remember to cancel the subscription. If he renewed it later, it would be at a later time on his own for his own reasons.

Maria turned once more to await him patiently. Now he had an image of doing something other than weeping on her shoulder.

Not trusting himself to speak, he turned to the bookcase and took down a small brass elephant bookend. It was nice work, but every time he looked at it he could see Vera cooing to the French merchant in Lyons. Bent forward, cleavage very much on show, "her best bargaining position" she always called it. Had she slept with him too? He cast the thought aside and handed the elephant to Maria.

No longer supported, several books fell over. He flopped the first six books on their side and shoved them over as an impromptu bookend.

"What's next?" She returned to stand stalwartly at his elbow.

It was a slow process at first, but one that picked up pace quickly. Box and bag. A lot of bag. A small oil painting in hideous colors that had matched only the hideous price tag. Book gifts he'd never wanted to read to begin which started the "to sell without waiting" box. The runner on the oak table. Knickknacks. Where had all of the knickknacks come from?

Then he started at the front door and began working his way toward the picture windows along the other side of his condo. The office was purely his, no, there was that stupid picture. He was the only one in it, but he could feel her behind the camera. In the bathroom, the toothbrush mug.

How had she insinuated herself so far into his life? Fifteen years of marriage, the last three apparently rife with adultery, was how.

The bedroom, with its view of Queen Anne Hill to the north, was fairly clean. Some old hangers, some ties that he'd never wear again if his life depended on it, and a girlie lamp on the other side of the bed, all pink and fake Victorian.

Each item he identified was whisked from his hands before it could burn his fingers, gone.

He was hardly aware of Maria anymore. She had become an extension of his own thoughts, and a focus for them. With her beside him, he felt strong, able to deal. And with each item they removed, he felt a layer stripped clear. As if Maria were paring him down, peeling off the hard rind to expose...something.

The question of what might remain after the last Vera layers were gone was one he wouldn't contemplate at the moment.

Last was the kitchen.

The only part of Vera that was here, other than a few more mugs he could hardly bear to handle, was the espresso machine. A good one. It had been a Christmas gift, in a good year. He used it every day.

He turned to Maria and she must have seen the confusion on his face.

"Was it a good memory?"

He could only nod, a tightness in his throat had cut off any words.

He'd lost so much. He'd lost his image of a happy family and a happy home. Worse, he'd lost any hope of a happy version of himself. But the espresso machine was from before that time. Vera had given the machine to him when they couldn't afford it, by scraping together an entire year's worth of a dollar per day stuffed into a jar. He'd bought her a used DVD set of some British comedy she'd liked, and she'd given him one of the best home espresso machines made.

What was he supposed to do with that? So much gone. This too?

He slumped back against one of the cabinets and slid down to sit on the floor. Tired. It had been too much, like a knife driven into his guts. It might hurt like hell, but to remove it would hurt even worse. Some part of his past *had* to have had a purpose.

Maria settled to the floor beside him.

It was jarring. He thought of her as so beautiful and such a lady. Yet, other than her dress forcing her to sit with her legs folded neatly to one side, she was probably younger than he was. She said she'd had Angelo when she was young. That meant before twenty. She'd mentioned that her son was thirty. Maybe she was a year or so older than he was, though that was wholly impossible to credit. She looked and acted so much younger than he felt. Either way, he was sitting on the floor but it still felt strange to see her do so.

She bumped a shoulder against his. As if she were simply offering support. Which is exactly what she'd been doing for, he glanced at the kitchen clock, for almost two hours.

"I'm such a goddamn mess."

"You are."

He laughed, "At least you could not agree with me so readily." He could smell her, without even turning to face her. Warm and spice. Like a winter cider but fresh, so fresh. Like mint or apples on the air.

"I am sorry to tell you this, Hogan Stanford, but you are human. So, you are a mess. You are without choice in this." Her tone was completely matter of fact.

"But," he didn't know how to express it. "But you're so perfect."

"If you think that, Mr. Hogan Stanford, then perhaps it is time I was going."

"No! You can't. I need to figure this out first." He scrambled around in his brain for some way to not admit out loud what an utterly ridiculous pedestal he had her on. Of course she was human, he just hadn't thought it through until this moment. But he knew absolutely that he didn't want her to leave.

"It's a disguise, right?" He turned to her and they were face-to-face only inches apart. The closeness did nothing to change his opinion of her. Her dusky complexion, her thoughtful dark eyes, her outrageously thick hair were all as real as they'd been when she sat in her window like a painted Venus.

"What is a disguise?" Her voice was a little more than a whisper.

"Your perfection. You certainly had me fooled. Here I was

thinking you were the perfect woman, which is, as you've pointed out, of course totally impossible. So, I figure you must really be an alien in disguise. Am I right?"

She eyed him suspiciously, but couldn't fight back the smile that tugged at those full lips.

No longer able to think while this close to her, he leaned in and kissed her.

MARIA KNEW she should be shocked. She was, but not in a bad way. She'd been watching Hogan carefully as she helped him clear the apartment of the unwanted portion of his past. He was decisive. Not bull in a china shop like Russell or driven like Angelo into high-energy flurries that left her and everyone else around him, except apparently Jo, utterly exhausted.

Hogan was steady, made decisions quickly with little fuss.

Maria would have said his movements were elegant, but that wasn't quite right. What they were was immensely efficient. Never carry one thing when you could carry three. No returning to clean up what was left behind as pieces were removed, but rather fixing the space immediately. She'd have purged the place, then gone back and tried to figure out what to do with the mess she'd left behind. Hogan's condo looked as well organized as the moment she'd come in; no sign, except in the mounds covering the dining table, that there was substantially less of it.

What shocked her about Hogan's kiss was how good it felt, how natural. She barely knew the man.

For that matter, she barely knew the woman who slid a hand up to tickle her fingers through his hair. Not even with her boyfriend Angelo—the one who had seduced and left her before she was seventeen and for whom her son had been named—had she been so forward. And the men she'd chosen since coming to America, she'd chosen carefully and rarely.

Hogan eased back without pulling away.

"Do not you dare say you are being sorry," she whispered, her voice surprisingly husky.

"I'm not, trust me." His voice was in little better condition. Then he kissed her on the forehead. "Surprised, yes. At both of us. But sorry, not one little bit."

"Oh," Maria was a little surprised at both of them as well. She waved a hand toward where they were sitting. "You appear to have swept my feet out from under me."

"That too appears to be mutual. Hell of a place for a first kiss."

"Yes. Years from now we will be able to say, 'Well, we always had the kitchen floor'."

He laughed, a warm, deep sound that welcomed her in.

"You know," he kissed her forehead once more slowly. "You're doing a lousy job of ruining your disguise of being perfect."

"I will have to be working on that." But she wasn't going to work at it too hard. Not with how good it felt to be leaning up against him.

CHAPTER 7

"*And what then?*" *Perrin* leaned in close and eager.

Maria wasn't quite sure why she'd called Perrin for lunch. It was Monday and the restaurant was closed. She also hadn't expected Jo and Cassidy to show up as well, though she should have. They were so close that you couldn't call one without calling all three. Perrin's shop was nearby, Cassidy's office was in her home just a few blocks from the Market, and Jo was the Market's Managing Director, even if it was technically her day off as well.

The four of them sat upstairs at Lowell's Restaurant in the Market, a small table close against the windows facing the Sound. She and Perrin were splitting a Chicken Apple Salad, Jo and Cassidy a Grilled Vegetable Panzanella, a Tuscan rustic bread salad.

"He make me an espresso."

Perrin's eyes practically crossed in her confusion, or perhaps disappointment. "You didn't push him down on the floor and use his body until you couldn't stay conscious any longer?"

Maria could hear Cassidy and Jo trying to leap in and cover

for her. But they didn't understand yet that Maria needed no protecting, especially not from Perrin.

"I think about it, but not yet."

Perrin didn't look away, as if Maria's sex life was the most interesting thing on the planet.

"But I knew a part of him wanted me to. So, I leave him something to think about."

"Ooo, Jo was right. You are scary smart." Perrin looked impressed. Impressed and thoughtful. She might do well with a little more thinking before she gave away her heart next time.

"So, espresso?" Cassidy went for the subject change.

"Yes, he had this beautiful machine that his wife had given him. He loved the machine, but he hates her connection to it. So I have him make me a decaf espresso which we drink with a delivered Chinese dinner."

"So…" Perrin leaned back in, clearly still eager for more details. "You connected it to you."

Maria supposed that she had, though that wasn't her intent. Then she considered what else had happened last night.

She'd enjoyed herself. Immensely.

Hogan had been both interested in her and interesting himself. They had talked late into the evening. He had tried to call a cab for her, she'd insisted on walking, wanted the fresh air to clear her head. He had insisted on walking with her, her hand comfortable in the crook of his arm as they strolled along.

At the front door to her building Hogan had proven two things. One, that he was an absolute gentleman; she'd had to be the one to kiss him. And second, that first kiss hadn't been a fluke at all. He was very gentle, but he was also very thoughtful. She could practically hear his brain working on how to improve the kiss moment by moment. Maria had let him, simply enjoying the experience. She'd hoped for electricity and had actually found the lightning she'd asked for.

Maria Parrano had gone to bed alone, but very content with the world.

"Better he connects with me than that awful woman. I do not have the knowing of what she did to him, but it must have been horrid."

"Damaged goods," Perrin nodded sagely. "They can be so much fun to fix up."

Maria nodded to let Perrin have the round, but it wasn't what she was thinking.

Hogan Stanford wasn't damaged, but she'd wager he wasn't often understood. Probably not even by himself, perhaps especially not. He was absolutely forthright. What he said, he was.

His words fit him.

If he disagreed with someone, he'd say it, often so bluntly that it sounded offensive, but it wasn't. Because when he agreed, he was just as blunt and to the point. Other than his occasionally quirky sense of humor, he was exactly as he appeared to be.

Jo and Cassidy had turned to a discussion of the latest bizarre-spouse behavior that their men were exhibiting.

Maria interrupted, "To quote Julia Morgan when talking about Angelo and Russell: They are perfect. Because they are perfectly themselves."

"That, Maria, is absolute truth," Jo agreed. The two girls continued comparing notes over their salad.

"Perfect?" Just like Hogan, she thought to herself. Perfectly himself.

"What was that?" Only Perrin had overheard Maria's whisper to herself.

"That is what Hogan Stanford said I was."

Perrin studied her for a long moment, and then wrapped Maria in one of her open-hearted hugs and kissed Maria on the cheek.

"Of course you are. If he didn't see that in you, he wouldn't deserve you."

Maria held onto her for an extra moment. Now she knew exactly why she'd called Perrin.

HOGAN MET HER, as promised, right after he was finished with volunteering at the shelter.

Maria had offered to make him dinner, but he'd insisted that he had that covered and she should dress warmly. She waited for him outside the shelter, not minding the chilly air, though she had worn slacks and a bright knit vest under her coat. Seattle's damp chill was still not as penetrating as the deep cold of New York City winters.

"You're here!" Hogan came up beside her, his face still bright from the kitchen's heat.

"You thought I would not be?"

He kissed her quickly, though not the least perfunctorily, taking the initiative this time, which she liked. He lingered long enough to heat her blood like a schoolgirl's and then began leading her down Yesler Way toward the waterfront.

"I thought that I had made it all up and you couldn't possibly be real. Do you have any idea what it was like to wake up in my apartment without all of Ver—herself's detritus in it?"

He gave her an effusive hug whirling her around three times until her own head was spinning and she actually needed his arm to stabilize herself.

"You're a miracle!" He practically shouted it to the sky. "I dealt with everything last night. After you left, I took out all of the garbage, dropped the books off here at the shelter, and that last box of questionable stuff is down in my basement storage locker. I'm free!" He shot his arms above his head for a moment as if scoring a goal.

His transformation was startling. As if someone had taken away the Hogan Stanford that she was just starting to know and replaced him. He continued to guide her along the evening-lit streets, his left hand clasped warmly over where her own was tucked in his right elbow, she allowed herself to bask in his new-found energy.

Nor was she immune to the compliment of his constant glances in her direction. No woman could be.

"There's something terribly touristy, that any self-respecting local boy could never admit to wanting to do. But taking his girl on a date, that's a good enough excuse, isn't it?"

'His girl?' Maria could barely catch her breath. He made her feel absolutely giddy. "What happened to the Hogan Stanford I met only yesterday?"

"Only yesterday? Wow! That can't be right." He stopped for a moment to blink at her like a surprised owl caught unexpectedly in a searchlight. "Yesterday? And I just kissed you like…" He trailed off uncertainly.

She thought about repeating her warning to not say he was sorry. She didn't want to be with a man who was sorry that he'd kissed her and made her feel so wonderful and desirable. Instead, she pulled him down to her and kissed him long and hard. He barely hesitated, wrapping her tight against him as they stood in the middle of a busy Seattle sidewalk.

They were quiet when they started walking again. It was as if they'd both gone too far and yet neither had gone far enough. She finally had to speak, to say something.

"You're right. Yesterday can't be right. If we met just yesterday then I would be a wanton hussy and you a hustler."

"I dunno. A hustler?" He nodded to himself. "Never been accused of that, but it sounds kind of cool, doesn't it?"

"I have no desire to be a hussy."

"Couldn't if you tried," was his immediate response. "Too much of the lady in you."

They continued until they crossed beneath the towering Seattle Viaduct. Two tiers of highway, each three lanes wide, that dominated the Seattle Waterfront. He had to speak up for her to hear him over the traffic noise.

"I don't know if I'll recognize Seattle when this comes down next year. My dad talked about this being built when he was kid. That would have been the fifties I guess."

The change to the Seattle skyline would be dramatic. It was presently dark and dingy beneath the towering roadway. But old factories were being replaced with boutique stores in anticipation. The change was happening slowly, but it was coming. Soon they would all be exposed to the sunlight and the waterfront would bloom.

They crossed Alaskan Way and reached the broad sidewalk that ran in front of the piers, stretching off down the entire Seattle waterfront. Just two nights ago she had said to the other members of the Fearsome Foursome that she was open to change. Suddenly, everywhere she turned, change appeared to be confronting her.

"So, Mr. Whatever-you-have-done-with-Hogan, what is this terribly touristy thing?"

Like a conjuring magician, he waved his hand to the left. They stepped clear of the cheerfully jostling crowd at the outdoor counter of the Crab Pot Seafood Bar, busy despite the cold.

There, rising above the end of the old wooden pier soared Seattle's newest wonder. The Seattle Great Wheel towered seventeen stories above the waterfront. The massive Ferris wheel, sporting thousands of white lights and dozens of gently swaying gondolas, commanded the waterfront.

Maria looked up at Hogan, who had paused to await her reaction.

"You are right. It is terribly touristy. So, Mr. Stanford, if we get a gondola alone, what kind of a good time are you planning to show 'your girl'?"

That got the expected blush and made her feel rather better.

He'd just confirmed that the real Hogan Stanford hadn't gone anywhere at all.

THEY DID INDEED GET their own gondola, not much of a crowd appeared on a Monday evening in early December. Three times around the Great Wheel, just the two of them. Maria knew exactly how horrified Perrin would be that they didn't make some use of their unexpected privacy, but the view out the window was too spectacular.

They sat side-by-side on the padded bench seat, comfortably holding hands. First, they climbed toward the city. It revealed itself in layers, first Alaskan Way running along the waterfront, then the double-deck of the Viaduct, until it too lay far below. Finally the city itself, its soaring skyscrapers like torches lighting the night sky, striving ever upward.

"It is such a young city," Maria gazed out at the shining skyscrapers. So many of them clearly born just in that last few decades.

"Are you implying that we aren't?"

"I am still young," Maria laughed. "There is too much life still ahead for me to feel any other way. How about you?"

He kissed her on the temple then turned back to the view. "You make me feel as foolish as when I was twenty. It's quite an odd feeling. Had you asked me a week ago, I might have told you just how ancient I was feeling. But from the moment I saw you a dozen stories below, I began to understand that I was alive for the first time in far too long."

As they reached the apex of the Ferris wheel, Maria tried not to feel uncomfortable. First, just how long had he been spying on her before she'd noticed him hovering beyond her take-out window? He was sounding a bit like a stalker.

Second, she was no one's savior. She was no great heroine.

And the man who saw her that way was due for a future letdown of immense proportion. Did she want to be around for that? For the chaos of his emotions? The fall was a long way down. The pity was that she liked him a great deal and didn't want to have to put up barriers between them.

Perhaps detecting her thoughts, Hogan leaned his shoulder gently against hers increasing their connection.

She considered pulling back, but was stopped by his soft voice, barely louder than the sighing of the wind around the gondola car and the gentle creak of its bearings.

"I'm not crazy, Maria. It is not because of you that I realized this, at least not really you."

"You're making even less sense than usual, Hogan."

She could see his silhouette nodding in the dark as they started down. The wheel reached well out over the water of Elliot Bay, a vast darkness below lit only occasionally by ferries and other small boats.

"I know. I'm good at that, aren't I?" He made it sound as if he were a little boy fishing for a compliment.

Maria laughed dutifully, but didn't feel it.

"What I saw from my high window that drew me out into the world again was a tourist walking through the Market. I didn't know anything about her, might even have been a flamboyant man. She, I'll say the person was a she, could have been eighteen or eighty. All I knew was that in a city of grays and blacks and REI jackets, she stood out. She wore a sky-blue wool coat down to her calves and the brightest gold hat I've ever seen. I spent a week walking the Market, looking to once more find that flash of color. To find the woman who would dress so brightly and uniquely."

He pointed out a shining ferry leaving dock from just a few piers down. It sparkled on the dark water. Maria knew they shared the same thought of it being pretty enough to point out, but not wanting to interrupt the conversation. Such simple communication between them. Perhaps he wasn't really all that strange.

"That whole week I spent looking and hoping, simply wanting to see how alive someone like that must appear up close. Knowing there was little or no chance of finding her, still I searched. What I realized was that I was searching for something more important. I'd lost a piece of myself somewhere. Lost it so badly that I had to wander about pretending I could find it somewhere other than within myself."

Maria liked this story. Could feel his absolute involvement in it. This wasn't some tale a man told to a woman he was interested in. This wasn't a stalker who had followed her, he was a man looking for himself. He was working it out even as they swung down closer and closer to the departing ferry.

"I don't know who it was that I saw from my high window. There's no way for me to tell, but I like to think that it was you."

Maria kept her lips tightly pressed together. The coat and hat he had described were indeed hanging in her closet, though she'd never thought of them as anything special.

"By the time I spotted you in your Botticelli window—"

"My what?" She turned to study him as they swung through the lights at the bottom of the wheel's arc and started their second journey around the wheel.

"That's how you look. Didn't you know? Right down to the simple golden frame around your window at Angelo's. I thought it was familiar, so looked it up online. It's almost a perfect match for the one around Botticelli's *Allegory of Spring* hanging in Florence."

She was going to kill Russell. Maria had just thought it was pretty wood trim. But of course Mr. World-famous-photographer Russell, who had such an amazing eye for art and composition, would have known exactly what he was doing when he had so kindly offered to set her up with a way to sell breakfast treats and gain new customers for Angelo's restaurant. She'd have to check the outside wall to make sure there was no little "description of the image" plaque bolted up as if she were hanging in a museum.

"Anyway, at that moment, I didn't care if I found that lady or not. For what I saw before me was a woman who clearly understood that life was a gift. It's something I lost sight of, maybe long ago."

They climbed once more into the city's night sky. But Hogan wasn't watching it. He was staring out the window as if desperately searching for some earlier version of himself.

"Maybe that's what Vera took out of me. Sorry, I know I'm not supposed to mention her."

"I give you dispensation this one time," she kept her voice gentle, not wanting him to stop.

He nodded his acknowledgement but his attention was still far away. "I'm not sure though. Maybe it was partly the job. Or a combination of things, some good, some bad. I had to see someone who reveled in the light, reveled in life itself to remind me of what was so important. You do that. It is so rare, so special, how could you not draw me like a beacon."

Now he turned to face her, so close she could see his eyes clearly despite the dim lighting of the waterfront falling behind them as they again swung downward.

"From now on I want to surround myself with people who think being alive is a gift. It has essential importance. I now see that Eric, the man who founded the shelter I volunteer at, has that. You have that. All I can hope to do is find some of that joy in myself and share that as well."

Maria tried to still her pounding heart. Tried to keep her reaction inside her, hidden, to how wonderful a man sat beside her.

She didn't remember the third turn of the Great Wheel at all. Her knees were weak and her lips ever so pleasantly sore as Hogan led her off the Ferris wheel and took her to dinner.

CHAPTER 8

"Are you okay, Mama?"

Maria blinked hard then looked down at what she'd been cooking. The ginger jam that she'd been simmering had scorched. A *bagnomaria* of chocolate had overheated and separated, which was exactly what the double boiler was supposed to prevent. She hadn't done that since she was a little girl standing on a kitchen chair to help her grandmother cook.

"Fine. I'm fine." She began cleaning up the mess. A glance at the clock said that she still had time if she stayed focused. Which would be much easier if she weren't so preoccupied by memories of how Hogan had made her body feel on that third time around the Ferris wheel. Men had fondled her breasts, but Hogan had worshipped them with his hands. He'd scooped her into his lap and run his lips down her neck and his hands over her body until—

"Mama?"

Angelo stood close beside her. A worried look on his face. She patted his cheek and insisted she was fine. He eyed her carefully before slowly rejoining Manuel on the cook line. They were experimenting on a dish for the new restaurant.

Angelo's Tuscan Hearth, which actually leaned more toward Ligurian fare, was primarily seafood. Liguria lay north of Tuscany, a thin slice of the coast, but it was lesser known. So, Angelo and Russell had named it for the more popular Tuscany. The new restaurant, Angelo's Piedmont Hearth, was a concession to the American clientele rather than the Italian "Piemonte." It would have a whole new menu, based on the stronger-bodied wines of the mountains and the meatier fare of the region.

Maria began scouring the pots quickly. By the time she'd turned back to the cook line, Graziella was there laying out fresh ginger, sugar, and chocolate.

"I know that look, Ms. Parrano."

"What look?" Maria did her best to sound innocent and knew she failed miserably.

"The same look that I saw in the mirror this morning."

Maria inspected her and now saw it blooming out of her. How had Maria missed it, the girl was radiant. A glance at the cook line showed Manuel was completely focused on his cooking. How was it that Graziella looked radiant, Manuel was totally in control, and she was an absolute distracted mess with the attention span of a parakeet?

Graziella must have noticed her attention and her scowl. "He fouled the sauce twice before Angelo came in. This is his third try."

Maria laughed and felt much better.

"He is treating you well?"

"Rosebuds. It's December and he gave me rosebuds." The young woman's smile and sigh was confirmation enough of what else had gone right. "When do we meet the man putting that smile on your face?"

Maria focused on coarse-chopping the chocolate while Graziella rebuilt the honey-based sugar syrup for the jam.

"Oh, I know him already, don't I? Your special customer. The one Manuel cooked breakfast for. Your charity case?" She turned it into a question of surprise.

"Hogan Stanford is being many things, but I discover that a charity case he is not. At least not the way I thought he was."

"Who is Hogan Stanford?" Russell snapped a photo with that fancy camera of his.

"Where did you come from?" Maria hadn't heard him come in and didn't know why he was aiming his camera at her. He shifted to the side for a different angle and she threatened him with the chocolate-coated wooden spoon she'd been using to stir with. He took the picture, of course, though he did back off a step.

"I came from New York. But you know that. Not getting forgetful in your dotage, are you, Ms. Parrano?"

"Just because you turned out so tall and handsome and I can no longer lay you over my knee, do not think that my spoon is any slower." She had used it frequently to whack him on the knuckles when he and Angelo were young and constantly trying to snatch bits from her cooking pot before they were served.

Graziella stirred the forming syrup to make sure that it heated evenly and didn't foam, "Can I have a demonstration? It sounds like a useful skill."

"I am here by invitation, Maria," Russell insisted. He backed off another step, just in case she decided to carry out her threat, and ran into a dish rack with a large clatter.

"We thought that to advertise the new restaurant, we should introduce the people behind the swinging doors. 'From our kitchen to your table' kind of feel. Make it personal. I wanted to start with two amazingly beautiful women, you know, sex appeal and all that." He gave a knowing leer that looked quite comical because they all knew how besotted he was by Cassidy.

Maria had to admit that it was a fine idea and didn't mind the compliment even though it was just so much *fesserie*. And while she didn't like having her picture taken unawares, she knew Russell would make her look so pretty that she wouldn't recognize herself. And with young and glowing Graziella beside her, Maria expected it would come out very well indeed.

"So, who is Hogan Stanford?" He snapped a picture of her protest, but it didn't save his knuckles from a quick rap.

HOGAN WAS IMPRESSED with himself when he visited Maria's window. He didn't hesitate, or avoid, or have to walk around the block three times. He simply queued up with the others, and other than a brief flash of a smile shared with Maria, he became just another customer waiting his turn. Someone was moving around snapping photos with a very high-end camera. Publicity photos maybe. Hogan almost felt as if he'd look like he fit into the scene.

The December morning was clear and cold, at least for Seattle, upper-thirties. Maria had selected a sweater of soft gray. It was all vertically ribbed, emphasizing the trimness of her waist and her exceptionally fine figure. Who was he kidding with that? Fine figure indeed. As if he were a priggish poet given to abundant alliteration.

Her magnificent breasts. He could feel his cheeks warm even as he thought the words, but to call them less wouldn't be appropriate either. Not for the man who had just last night so appreciated their texture, the way they fit the curve of his palm, how they had responded to his attentions aboard the gondola. They were not overlarge, but were rather emphasized by that slender waist he could practically wrap his two hands fully around.

He allowed his attention to drift. Her neck, the clean lines of her well-defined Italian chin, and lips that he knew were so soft and opened with a soft sigh when…

"Hogan?"

He had progressed to the front of the line without noticing. That is, without noticing anything except how she looked.

"You look incredible."

"Your Botticelli?"

He rapped his knuckles lightly against the gilded window frame in answer.

"Have you had breakfast yet?"

When he shook his head, she set out a coffee and a *cornetto*. He made a show of carefully counting out three one-dollar bills, she'd teased him mercilessly about only having hundreds in his wallet.

"Are you free this evening?" It felt so normal, asking his girl out.

"Come to my condo after you are done at the shelter, I make you a nice dinner. Now shoo. You block other customers."

He glanced behind, and there were several people behind him.

"And you too are so pretty that you are distracting me terribly," she said more softly.

He turned back startled. "Did I hear that right?"

She made shooing motions. When he moved off, she called him back to take his breakfast. Okay, maybe he didn't fit in completely. But the coffee was warm in his hands and Maria's smile was warm as well.

He moved off down Post Alley and turned downslope toward the park to enjoy the morning sunshine as he ate his breakfast. It overlooked Elliot Bay, which was an amazing sight on a sunny morning. He'd also be able to see the Ferris wheel and think about—

"Hogan Stanford?" The voice sounded buddy-buddy. A moment later someone clamped a hand over Hogan's shoulder. Hard. He looked over and up. It was the photographer from outside the restaurant, and he was a big man: tall, broad-shouldered, cliché-handsome. His camera was still clamped in his other hand.

"Uh, yes?"

"So, Hogan. Tell me how you've been doing, buddy?"

Hogan tried to wrench his shoulder free. Managed it on the second try without dislocating anything or losing his *cornetto*. This guy looked easy-going, but his grip had been anything but.

"Uh fine. Would you care to tell me who the hell you are?" The man's confrontational approach had taken Hogan back to one too many corporate meetings. He could feel his spine stiffen and his professional assuredness slip over him like an extra winter cloak.

"Maybe," the photographer looked at him as if there was no maybe about it. "We can work out a trade on that one."

They descended the steep half-block to Pike Place. They crossed the street together into the park at the north end of the Pike Place Market as if seeking a suitable site for the upcoming battle.

It was still too early for the homeless who worked the park once the tourists came out, so the area was mostly empty. A small ring of grass trapped behind a low concrete wall and a wide walking area.

Without Hogan quite being sure how, they ended up side by side, leaning on the steel rail that overlooked the viaduct roaring with morning rush hour traffic and the bay beyond. Sure enough, there was the Ferris wheel off to his left. But to his right…

"So," Hogan faced the big man. "Time to answer the question, or do I call over that friendly policeman?" He nodded to the man enjoying coffee and a cheese Danish a dozen feet farther along the rail.

The big guy glanced over his shoulder. "Rent-a-cop, night security. Won't help you a bit, but you don't need protection from me. At least not yet."

"Oh. And why is that?" He did his best to sound disdainful, impressing even himself.

"I..." the guy rubbed a hand over his face. And in the process almost erased the big bruiser expression from his face. He actually looked fairly pleasant as he continued. "Damn! I'm screwing this up, but I gotta ask. Are you the Hogan Stanford who is putting that expression on Maria Amelia Avico Parrano's face?"

"What expression?" So, this was about Maria somehow. Was she part of some mafia organization?

"The goofy one."

Hogan inspected the photographer again. He didn't look like some mob enforcer. He looked like someone you'd see on the cover of *GQ*. A goofy expression?

"I can only hope it's me." Hogan admitted. He really liked the idea that he wasn't the only one feeling totally ridiculous every time thoughts of last night came to mind, which was constantly.

"Aw shit."

"What? And who are you?"

"Russell. I'm Russell Morgan. Maria is kind of like my mother, except I have a mother too. That sounded even stupider than usual."

Russell and Angelo. Maria had talked over dinner last night about raising the two boys.

"Where's your *consigliere?*"

"Who? Oh, Angelo. Fretting over some new venison morel-mushroom sauce. Okay, maybe I'm coming across a little heavy. But nobody has ever made Maria mess up in the kitchen, ever. Nor put that smile on her face. Angelo didn't see it. I probably wouldn't have without my camera. It shows things." He did something with the controls on the back, flicked through the images, and then held it up for Hogan to see.

Just moments ago: Maria sitting in the window, serving the person ahead of Hogan. The shot was mostly from behind Hogan, his own face was hidden, he was more of a soft blur in the foreground giving the impression of a longer line than there'd actually been at the moment.

Then Russell selected the next photo.

Hogan was now at the window, still from behind. And Maria's face had lit up with that brilliant smile of hers. The one that made him think of sunny days and laughing women.

"Oh." It was all he could think to say. He hadn't seen the change, he'd been too busy being happy to see her, even if just for that moment. That he had been the one to cause that change utterly floored him. He tried to think of something more intelligent to say, but failed completely.

"So, why are you after her?" Russell turned the camera back off and slung it over his shoulder.

"Are you always this crass?"

Russell grimaced then shrugged. "Yeah, I guess. Ask my wife, she'd probably say I'm being a jerk, but I…"

He trailed off and Hogan decided to help him. "You're just being protective."

Russell nodded.

"Well, I'm glad that she has people to protect her. Though she doesn't strike me as someone who needs much protection."

Russell rubbed a hand over his knuckles as if they hurt. "You don't know the half of it."

They spent a pleasant hour looking out at the bay and getting to know each other. He was getting to like Russell, who clearly adored Maria. He'd made his own success and walked away to discover himself.

And in the process Russell had fallen in love.

It was something they had in common. Neither of them had to ever work again, but they weren't built that way. They had to do something. Hogan had lost that, but was slowly rediscovering it at the shelter.

Maria was right, Russell was a good boy. Twenty years Hogan's junior and madly in love with his wife.

Hogan didn't know squat about wines, but even he had heard of Cassidy Knowles. A food-and-wine critic who had dropped out to create a wine cooperative of the vineyards of Washington State. She wasn't aiming her sights at keeping Washington as one of the nation's top three wine regions, along with Oregon. Her ambition just might be to unseat Napa from the pinnacle.

A particularly fine sloop cruised along the waterfront. That got them onto one of Hogan's favorite subjects, sailboats.

"You're a sailor? Shit! How am I supposed to despise you if you're a sailor?" Russell's protest was vehement enough to turn heads of the first tourists of the morning, also leaning against the cold metal rail to watch the world go by.

"Life is tough, isn't it?"

"Got a boat?"

"Did," Vera had hated sailing, so he'd finally let it go. Maybe it was time to look for a new boat. "Just a little cruiser, a Tartan 34. Miss her on days like this. Clear, good breeze."

Russell was just nodding in sympathy. A non-sailor would make some remark about a thirty-four-foot boat not being small. A beginner would be impressed by the Tartan, she'd been a very classy boat. But someone who sailed bigger boats would simply understand. You could go deep sea in a thirty-four if you didn't mind getting slapped around a bit. But what she was made for was just knocking around places like the Mediterranean and Puget Sound, maybe up the Inside Passage to Alaska, something he'd always meant to do, but hadn't.

"You?"

"Yeah. Honey of a boat out at Shilshole Marina. She's a one-of-a-kind fifty-footer. Full keel, just ten-foot-six on the beam."

"Fast." Hogan remarked. A proof that he knew his boats, a compliment to Russell for choosing a boat that was about the sailing more than the comfort, and no comment on the length that showed he knew more than simply the numbers about boats. Whatever her condition, the speed would be the most notable factor in a craft that size.

Russell's phone beeped. He answered.

"Yeah, down at the park rail." He glanced over at Hogan. "How's your coffee?"

Hogan shook it to show that it was long gone empty, then he chucked it in a nearby can.

Russell spoke once more into the phone, "Bring an extra." Then he hung up.

They continued talking about boats they had each admired.

"HEY, ANGELO. GIVE ME MY COFFEE."

Hogan turned to face the new arrival. This would be Maria's son and he was very interested in meeting him.

Where Russell was several inches taller than Hogan, Angelo was a couple inches shorter, though almost as broad-shouldered. He wore a white chef's coat open at the throat, apparently glad for the cold air after the kitchen's heat. He had those dark Italian good looks that made all women swoon. He was the male version of his mother's intense beauty. No doubting their relationship.

Hogan wondered if there was any of the father in Angelo other than his build. Looking at the two men together, Hogan wondered how Maria had survived raising them.

"Angelo, Hogan. Hogan, Angelo."

They shook hands then Angelo handed over a fresh coffee.

"Where's my *cornetto*?" Russell demanded.

"Dude, Mama sold out half an hour ago. You gotta be quicker than that."

"Shit!" Russell cursed.

Hogan decided to salt the wound. "It was crazy good. Some ginger-chocolate-strawberry mix that shouldn't have worked but was amazing."

Russell groaned and knocked back a big swallow of coffee then was gasping out great clouds of steam into the chill air as he cursed, then sipped again more cautiously.

"So, you like my mama's cooking? I like you already, Hogan."

Russell glanced at Hogan then shot him a wicked grin before facing Angelo. "He likes a lot more than her cooking, buddy boy."

"Huh? What?"

Russell rolled his eyes at Angelo's denseness. "Your mama's got a new boyfriend, one Hogan Stanford."

Hogan wanted to be pissed at Russell for making the news a total bomb drop, but couldn't quite work it out. First, he'd pretty much deserved that for ribbing Russell about the *cornetto*. And it was going to have to come out at some point, he'd just have preferred that it was Maria dealing with it rather than him. Assuming the relationship even went anywhere. Hoping it did.

Angelo turned slowly, like a bull getting ready to charge, until he faced Hogan square on.

"What was that?"

"Yep!" Russell cheerfully overran anything Hogan might have said. "Pretty far along, too, is my guess looking at both of them. Don't punch him, Angelo. Can't be hurting those famous hands of yours."

"Punch him? I'm going to rip him limb from bloody limb."

"If you do," Hogan figured he better say something quick. "You'll end up dropping your coffee. Your mother makes pretty good coffee. It would be a real pity to waste it."

Angelo blinked, now like a bull faced with a red cape held by a rodeo clown that he had no idea what to do with.

Russell snorted out a laugh. "I know. Lot to take in, isn't it? She's hot stuff, Angelo, we've known that since before we grew our first mustaches trying to piss her off. It was only a matter of time before some damn male on the planet wised up to what a dish she is."

Hogan could appreciate what Russell was doing. Having precipitated the whole upset for his own amusement, he was now redirecting Angelo's attention away from Hogan. While he appreciated it, he would fight his own battles.

"She's an amazing woman, Mr. Parrano. She loves you very much you know."

Russell nodded, "She does, Angelo, though the lord alone knows why."

"You too actually, Russell." His observation didn't slow the man down a bit.

"Makes her judgment pretty suspect, don't you think? What about it, Hogan? You gonna trust a lady who loves the two of us like sons? Gotta be something wrong with her."

Angelo chucked his coffee aside, hauled back, and unleashed a huge punch.

Hogan flinched even though it was Russell's arm that took the brunt of the blow. Russell barely rocked back on his heels when it landed.

Russell laughed. Then, after making a smooth hand-off of his coffee cup to Hogan, he wrapped Angelo into a headlock and began rapping his knuckles on Angelo's head—hard.

"Hello! Hello in there!" Russell was practically shouting in Angelo's ear, then he winked at Hogan. "Just think, Angelo. Maybe they've already had sex."

Hogan shook his head in denial and Russell rolled his eyes sadly, as if marking Hogan a fool.

Angelo struggled briefly once more before giving up. He

mumbled, "Aw shit!" somewhere in the vicinity of Russell's armpit then finally relaxed.

Hogan felt sorry for him when Russell let him up.

Russell reached for his coffee, but Hogan handed it to Angelo.

"Hey!" Russell protested.

Angelo merely sneered at him and drank from the cup. "Best man wins."

"That would be me then," Hogan said.

Both men turned to look at him speculatively.

"First, of the three of us," he knew he was risking danger with this one. "I'm the only one who hasn't been beaten on this morning."

"That we can fix," Angelo offered, but there wasn't much heat behind it.

"Second, I figure I'm safe because I can't see either of you explaining to Maria that you beat me up on our very first meeting."

"Damn, Angelo," Russell stole back his coffee. "This guy's smart. We're gonna have to be sneaky."

"Third," now he had both of their attentions. "I win because I'm the one who has a date tonight with Maria Amelia Avico Parrano."

Russell grinned, "Got us there, my short Italian friend, doesn't he?"

Angelo groaned.

CHAPTER 9

"*H*ogan?" *Maria looked aghast* at the three men entering the restaurant's back door. She'd dreaded this moment, having no idea how she was going to tell Angelo about her boyfriend. Or whatever she was going to call Hogan.

She started to feel relief that it had occurred without her, but decided they wouldn't be laughing together if the two boys knew. Maybe Hogan had somehow identified and befriended them both to make it easier. She had no idea what was going on.

"Maria!" Hogan called out happily. Dropping a to-go cup into the garbage, he walked up to her. No, he swaggered, looking immensely male and pleased with himself. Just steps before he reached her station he winked at her broadly.

Then he kissed her. Not a little kiss, but one that shifted her from bewildered to melting. She could feel his smile turn just a little wicked.

"I told you, Angelo, and I told you," she became vaguely aware of Russell's teasing tone over the buzzing in her ears. "Parents have sex, too. Lucky for us or we'd never have been born."

Angelo whimpered quietly.

She pushed Hogan aside and saw that they had quite the audience. Russell had an arm draped over her son's shoulders, perhaps holding him from charging at Hogan, perhaps merely keeping him upright. Graziella stood by the kitchen door and looked even more melty than she had this morning. Manuel, the *sous chef,* and Nora beside him, were grinning at their boss' complete confusion.

A couple of the other line cooks were applauding. Marko, the young dishwasher, was the only one apparently sharing Angelo's state of shock. She was becoming a second mother to the teen and apparently Ms. Parrano with a boyfriend was more than he could imagine.

Russell shook Angelo in a friendly fashion. "Maybe parents only have really bad sex, leaving all the good sex for us young studs." Russell winked in Hogan's direction.

Hogan had slid a hand around her waist, and appeared far too pleased with himself.

Maria grabbed a wooden spoon and whacked Hogan on top of the head.

"Hey! What? Ow!"

"You! You get out of my kitchen. You already mess up my food once this morning. Out! Out! Before you make me mess up even more." She chased him to the back door.

Then just before he ducked through to escape, she stopped him with a hand on his jacket. Two could play at this game.

She pulled his head down into a kiss and let herself flow against him. He felt so good, it was impossible. But it was so very real at the same time.

Then she scooted him out the door with a soft, "Shoo!" and a slap of her wooden spoon on his backside for good measure.

Maria turned back, and squared her shoulders to face whatever the consequences were.

Angelo came up and took both her hands. He squeezed them hard and looked her right in the eye.

"Does he make you happy, Mama?"

She shrugged. Happy was such a small word for how Hogan Stanford made her feel. "Yes, Angelo. He does so far."

He didn't speak, but merely wrapped her in a fierce hug. Over his shoulder she could see Russell grinning at them.

Maria tried not to cry, but she'd raised two such good boys that she couldn't help herself.

"Tonight, I am cooking you a special dinner."

Maria's apartment had been overflowing with wondrous smells when he arrived.

Once she'd buzzed him through the locked door, it could have been a different world though he was just two blocks from the shelter. Seattle was like that. It was a small enough city that shelters backed onto art galleries and condos towered above seedy bars which were just two doors down from a good French restaurant in one direction and a narrow *Pho* noodle shop in the other.

Her condo was on the seventh floor, well above the vibrant mix of the Pioneer Square evening. Even in the night he could see that she had a decent view over the viaduct to the Sound. When that came down in a year or so, it would be magnificent. The contractor had done an excellent job on the sound insulation, he couldn't hear the roadway much at all.

The furnishings were not fancy or complex, IKEA mostly. "They were Angelo's," Maria explained. The kitchen, however, was magnificent.

"Also Angelo's." His observation earned him a smile of unbounded pride from Maria.

A red sauce was simmering gently on the back burner and filled the apartment with layers of olfactory wonders. It was a heady blend of tomato and spice and possibility.

They shared a glass of Barolo as he regaled her with tales of meeting Russell and Angelo. She set him to making tiny prosciutto bruschetta dressed with olive oil and fresh mozzarella. She formed meatballs with practiced, delicate gestures, and slid them into the sauce to cook.

He fed her a bruschetta and she kissed his fingers. He held a glass of wine for her to sip as she worked on the salad. A drop of wine caught at the corner of her lips and he kissed it away.

Her eyes were so dark when they looked up at him. Worlds were revealed there. Worlds of desire. And of hope.

Without a word, he moved to the stove and turned off the burner.

She washed her hands and was toweling them dry when he drove his fingers into her hair and kissed her. That soft sigh as her lips parted against his absolutely slayed him.

He went to lead her to the bedroom, though he didn't know which door to head for.

She undid the knot on her apron, and pulled it off over her head.

For the brief moment that gesture forced their lips apart, she whispered, "We will always be having the kitchen floor."

He lay her down on the smooth, polished oak. And then feasted upon her.

SPAGHETTI AND ITALIAN MEATBALLS, while sitting naked on the kitchen floor. Spumoni ice cream sandwiches in a hot shower, dripping cherry, pistachio, and chocolate flavors faster than they could eat them. They eventually had made love in the bed as well before collapsing into sleep.

Hogan rarely slept more than five hours. He awoke seven hours later when Maria's alarm went off. Thankfully, being a wise woman, she'd set it a little earlier than she really needed.

CHAPTER 10

*H*ogan hated missing *Maria's* breakfasts, but shifting his schedule at the shelter was worth it. Eric let him move to morning and lunch prep, with Monday and Tuesdays off so that his schedule matched Maria's. With the quality of the additional foodstuffs that arrived from Angelo's restaurant, only a day or two old, he could have asked for anything and Eric would have given it to him.

The shelter was being more fun as well. Richie was as weird as ever, but Hogan stopped being his primary target. He now shared that particular gift more equally with the other kitchen volunteers. Eric teased about making Hogan an honorary KP-private, after all, only on Army Kitchen Patrol did anyone have to peel so many potatoes.

Hogan knew the place hadn't changed, so it must be him. He supposed it made sense, because he certainly didn't recognize the Hogan Stanford of mere weeks ago whose favorite place was sitting quietly at his living room window. It was as if the Seattle he'd grown up in and always loved had come back to life for him.

Maria knew surprisingly little of Seattle, having only lived here for six months and spending most of that in her son's restaurant. And she certainly hadn't been here for a Christmas, so he led her to every ridiculous touristy thing to do. Seattle at Christmas was a wonderful city, even if there was a lack of snow except for one fine-dusted evening.

They stood in the chilly rain for half an hour to ride on the Christmas carousel that was set up on the Westlake Center mall each winter. Two grownups and hundreds of little kids with harried-looking parents in tow. The carousel was a spectacle of lights and joy. He rode a carved blue charger, and Maria beside him on a splendid lavender mare. They both giggled like they were six again.

He took her on quiet drives through neighborhoods known for their Christmas lights. He saved the "Garden d'Lights" show at the Bellevue Botanical Garden for an especially clear night with a half moon shining high in the sky. They had nearly frozen on the cold, clear night, but the stars had sparkled and the lights had glittered off her hair until he was quite assured that she was magical, no matter how often she denied it.

She had tickled Santa's beard at Macy's in the window below what every Seattleite worth his salt still called the Bon Star. It was a great white star that had shown down Third Avenue every December for decades despite the store's name change.

They rode the ferry from the Seattle waterfront over to Bainbridge Island. He took her to the Streamliner Diner, a 1950s classic of chrome, Formica, and leatherette bench seats. Their return trip through the mid-winter darkness had shown the glorious display of the Seattle skyline from the twin sports stadiums in the south to the Space Needle that still commanded the northern end of downtown.

There was one special thing that Hogan wanted to share with her, but for that he'd need a little help.

"Maria!" She turned from studying the dark waters of Elliot Bay at the call. Cassidy, Jo, and Perrin were trooping down the pier toward her. Hugs and surprise were shared all around.

"What are you all doing here?"

"We were hoping you knew. Russell was being awfully mysterious."

Maria shook her head, "Hogan too. He just said to meet him here."

"Hogan!" Perrin practically crowed with delight. "I told you that's why we hadn't seen her in so long. It's not that she decided we were too much trouble. So tell me. Tell me! Is he really wonderful? Was your first time on the Ferris wheel?"

The Seattle Great Wheel shone just a few piers to the south of where they stood.

"No, it was not on the Ferris wheel."

"So…" Perrin drew it out so dramatically that the other girls giggled, despite being overly serious women turning thirty. Perrin tipped her head ever so slightly saying that this would be a terrific opportunity to tease the others.

"The kitchen floor at my condo."

"Yes!" Perrin did a fist pump and danced a bit about the pier. Her white hair shining where it peeked out beneath a crazy knit hat. The hat was gray and covered with a line of what looked like tiny blue British police boxes.

Maria shared a moment of shock with Jo and Cassidy about what Perrin had just gotten her to admit, then they burst out laughing in unison.

"Don't worry, Maria," Jo gave her a hug. "Neither of us know how Perrin does it, but if it's about boys, don't ever think you can hide it with Perrin around."

Perrin switched over to an energetic shimmy that might have been a start of a conga line. Maria grabbed her waist and soon they were all dancing about the pier in the reflected city lights.

"Oh, look at that!" Perrin stumbled to a halt and they piled up behind her like a train wreck.

Just a few hundred feet off the end of the pier, a sailboat had turned toward them. Its rigging was festooned with brightly colored Christmas lights. Blues, golds, reds, and greens traced the line of the mast and where the sails would be if they weren't furled. The lights also swooped along the low, sleek lines of the hull and traced each window. A spiral of purple lights even wound around the tiller where several dark figures moved about the cockpit.

"It's beautiful!" Maria felt there was something familiar about the boat. She almost had it when Cassidy cried out.

"Hey! That's our boat!"

Russell's voice floated back to them over the water. "It is, my love."

In moments, the boat slid up at a landing beside the pier. The four women scrambled aboard, Hogan meeting them at the rail to offer a hand, and in moments, Russell was motoring out into Elliott Bay once more.

Cassidy hurried to the stern and leapt into Russell's arms. Had he been a lesser man, they'd have tumbled backward off the stern and into the freezing waters below.

Angelo popped his head up from below. "Who wants hot cider?"

Jo and Perrin went back to give a hand.

Hogan straightened from re-securing the lifeline, he'd dropped a section of it for them to climb aboard.

Maria pulled his face down to hers and kissed him. "An evening sail! What a lovely surprise."

He rubbed his hands very possessively from her shoulders to her hips and back. Any chills she'd felt waiting on the dock he banished as if they'd never been.

"Cut it out, you two," Russell called. "You'll just make Angelo nervous."

"And me sooo totally envious!" Perrin walked up to them carrying two steel cups with snap lids. She handed one to each and then hugged them both fiercely.

"Hi Hogan. I'm Perrin. And if I ever find out you don't appreciate Mama Maria enough, you're going overboard, winter or not. We clear?"

"Yes, ma'am." Hogan glanced at Maria for guidance as Perrin made the threat sound completely serious.

Maria left him to flounder. Like everyone else, he'd have to figure out on his own how to deal with Perrin.

"So," she winked at Maria before turning back to Hogan. "Kitchen floor, huh? Way to go you two." She gave him a friendly pat on the arm and headed back to the cockpit.

"Uh…" was all Hogan managed.

"I know," Maria empathized. "She does that to you."

"Is she married?"

"No, and do not be getting of any ideas."

"Huh? No, I didn't mean that. I was just wondering if we should observe a moment of silence on the behalf of whatever unsuspecting male she ultimately sets her sights on."

Maria kissed his cheek. "He will be most lucky man, whoever he is."

"Like me," Hogan hugged her tightly, then she led him back to the cockpit to meet her other friends.

"OH LOOK AT THAT ONE!" It was probably the tenth time Perrin had said that this evening. "It's so sweet!"

Hogan was very tempted to dismiss her as flighty, maybe even empty-headed. The others were careful of her. Perhaps careful *with* her would be more accurate. Protective, maybe overprotective.

Except Maria.

Perrin was the one Maria was most often beside, which told him that there was far more to the waif-like girl than appeared on the surface. Though it was clear that the three girls worshipped "Mama Maria" almost as much as Angelo and Russell did, it was Perrin who had threatened him. There was something special about her relationship with Maria.

Perrin was pointing off to starboard at the latest boat to join the Christmas Boat Parade. Every year, the boat parade would visit the various waterside communities from Tacoma to Seattle and all around Lake Washington and Lake Union. The lead boat was a tour boat and hosted a different choir each night. Tonight a gospel choir was belting out the carols, not really needing the speaker system. Their music carried clearly over the quiet waters.

The newest arrival at the tail of the boat parade wasn't much to look at. It was a couple on a small boat with a single strand of blue lights. He'd always found blue lights to be a little sad.

"They're so cute. Like a puppy dog just so happy to be here that they don't care how they look."

Hogan had looked at the same boat and seen someone who simply hadn't tried very hard. He liked Perrin's interpretation much better. Maybe he was starting to understand what Maria saw in her.

He turned from the boat and found that he was somehow seated hip to hip with Perrin in the cozy cockpit. By the bright Christmas lights that he'd spent an afternoon helping Russell put in place, he could see Perrin's soft blue eyes very clearly.

In that instant he finally understood; he was facing a deeply insightful intelligence masked behind a hyperactive smokescreen. He'd faced corporate executives who couldn't rouse such a focused and intent look.

"Single, divorced, or widowed?"

"Uh, divorced."

"Why?"

"I can't say."

"Can't or won't? Why? Is she famous, or an international spy?" Definitely still a layer of flighty there.

"No," Hogan shook his head. "I'm just not allowed to."

Perrin squinted at him for a long moment, then glanced over his shoulder and back.

"Mama Maria swore you to secrecy?"

Hogan opened his mouth to answer.

"No," she corrected herself. "She said it was bad for you to talk about your ex- or even think about her." Perrin didn't make it a question.

"How did you just do that?"

"What?"

"Answer a complex question correctly without a single fact."

She hit him with that flashing smile and a girlish grin. The flighty chick was back. "Magic."

He laughed, but stopped her from turning away with a light touch on her arm. "No, really."

Perrin sobered and inspected him carefully, then nodded to herself as if deciding something about him. This was a vastly different woman from the one he'd been speaking to just moments before.

"Maria said you'd been hurt, but she chose you. That means you're an amazing man because I know that she is scary smart about people. That's means you told her something, but now you can't tell me anything. So, she's trying to help you erase the past." Again that simple shrug, making her conclusion obvious. "I want to grow up to be just like her."

He took both her hands in his, figuring it was probably the only way to keep her focus on him. Then he kissed her on the cheek.

She blinked at him in confusion.

"You're on the right track. You're scary smart, too, Perrin."

"WHAT DID YOU DO TO HER?" Maria held Hogan's hand as they returned up the Pike Street Hill Climb to reach his condo. The Market was mostly closed, so they took the outside stairs at the south edge of the Market to enjoy the night. It was a long steady climb that slowly revealed the waterfront each time they stopped at a landing to look back at the way they'd come.

The boat parade had broken up. A few boats lingered, but most were headed back toward their berths. The girls had gone back with the two boys to return the boat to Shilshole Marina a few miles to the north. Not enough seats in the carpool for all of them to stay together, Hogan and Maria had been dropped back at the pier to walk the few blocks up the hill.

"What did I do to whom? Oh Perrin. Didn't do anything. I like her."

Maria watched Hogan, trying to read those thoughts he kept mostly to himself. After raising Angelo and Russell, she should be used to reticent men.

Of course, Angelo's father had been anything but reticent, he had talked at length about dreams, plans, and the future. None of which had happened. The moment she was pregnant, he was gone.

Perhaps reticent was a good thing. Hogan spoke, but mainly when he had something to say.

Having survived the gauntlet, he deserved some peace tonight.

He'd impossibly befriended Angelo and Russell; tonight they'd been as thick as thieves and comfortable together.

Hogan had also won Cassidy and Jo's probationary approval, not an easy task. She'd seen them double-teaming him several times on the boat. They were subtle, handing off questions mixed in idle conversation. Of course, she'd expect no less from two such successful women.

It was Perrin who surprised her. The evening had begun with Perrin threatening Hogan. Not long after, Maria had seen the two speak for just a few moments. Maria would have paid several secret recipes to overhear that conversation, but couldn't figure out how to do it. And it was over so abruptly she'd never had a chance to move closer.

Then Perrin had come over, hugged her, and whispered in her ear. "I'm going to start designing your wedding dress. You'll look incredible."

Then Perrin had given one of her shrug-off laughs and gone after more mulled cider, leaving Maria in such a state of shock she couldn't speak even when Angelo asked if she was okay.

Wedding dress? She'd seen the dresses that Perrin had designed for Cassidy and Jo's weddings and they were stunning. Cassidy's was already getting press for Perrin's Glorious Garb and Russell had designed a beautiful ad using it and the bridesmaids' dresses. He had a whole reveal campaign planned once Jo was married and Angelo could be allowed to see the dress.

But there was no chance that Maria was ready for a wedding dress. They'd only known each other for… That couldn't be right.

"Hogan, what date did you first come to my window?"

"December first. Why?"

She didn't say anything. It was too little time.

"Oh. December 14th. Our two-week anniversary. And I didn't get you a present. Bad Hogan. Bad Hogan." As if that were his new first name.

"A present?" Her voice was a choked squeak that had nothing to do with reaching the top step and broad landing at the head of the long climb.

"Well, either I owe you a present, or you're busy thinking what I'm thinking."

"And what is that?" Maria was almost afraid to ask.

Hogan turned her to face him.

The moon still shone in the sky above, the brighter stars showing despite the streetlights. Of the whole waterfront, only the Ferris wheel still towered above them, lit red and green in celebration of the season and the boat parade.

"I'm thinking how impossible it is that I've fallen in love in a mere fourteen days."

She heard the word come from his lips.

She knew that it reached her ears, because she heard it.

But it stalled somewhere before it reached her brain.

"Love?"

He nodded, almost sadly. Then he pulled her in and kissed her on the forehead. "I know. We had such a beautiful friendship going on here. Real pain in butt for me to go off and fall in love with you, isn't it? Throws in all sorts of complications. But true nonetheless."

"Complications?" She could barely understand what he was saying. Why did her brain choose that word to whisper? She should be saying— No, she shouldn't! Absolutely not! She was positively not ready to be saying that. Had said it to no one other than her boys since… Since she was a sixteen-year-old Italian girl who'd just lost her virginity.

"Yes. Now Angelo is going to have to figure out whether or not he really is going to kill me. Russell I think I can play the fellow-sailor card to buy my safety. Actually, he'd probably just sit back while cheering on both sides whichever way it goes. Jo and Cassidy will definitely escalate from tonight's efforts to a full Spanish Inquisition. Torture with soft pillows, comfy chairs, the whole nine yards of Monty Python. They're unbelievably cute when they think they're being subtle."

"And Perrin?"

Hogan pulled her into his arms and wrapped her tight and safe against him. He blocked any chances of shakes or terrors that she expected to be feeling. He nuzzled her hair briefly before whispering his response.

"Perrin. My best guess is that she'll be your maid of honor, holding the shotgun to my back just in case."

CHAPTER 11

*M*aria didn't know which way to turn. She couldn't call the girls. Each of their biases were clear. She certainly couldn't sit down with her son, and even less so with Russell. She wanted to call Julia Morgan, but she and her husband were somewhere in Australia, at least according to their last postcard. With her husband's retirement, the two of them had become world travelers.

It was ridiculous. She knew everyone in Pike Place Market, and had no one to talk to. Except Hogan. But he was the last person she was going to be talking to about…Hogan.

He'd been very patient and kind with her all week. Not demanding that she respond. Not insisting on the words. She couldn't imagine how it must hurt him. She wanted to say them, but each time she tried, they caught in her heart, bound there as if by chains.

She had loved and lost. It had gifted her a wonderful son and a wonderful life, but that early pain was still wound tightly deep in her breast.

At a loss, Maria finally went by Perrin's store. Her shop was nestled in the ground floor of an old brick building on Second Avenue just a few blocks north of the Market. Hogan told her that this whole area of Bell Town had totally transformed over the last decade. It had been the rundown edge of Seattle's downtown. Now it was the newest.

Tall condos had invaded only in a few places. But the old brick facades were cleaned up and in decent shape, filled with dozens of small entrepreneurs in every city block. Boutiques, both tiny and larger like Perrin's, were packed in among food vendors, tiny restaurants, dance clubs, bars, offices of creative design companies… It was an almost dizzying collection of youthful energy.

She ducked through the glass door of Perrin's Glorious Garb, a tinkling bell announcing her arrival. Maria always loved coming here, and not just for the amazing clothing. Perrin had taken over an old 1950s diner and turned it into a generous menu of bold options. The place had a light, cheerful feel that was a pleasure all in itself.

In one red leather booth, all of the tables had been removed to reveal the outfits, sat a trio of women mannequins clad in form-fitting attire. But it wasn't just some clingy fabric, not if Perrin designed it. The blouses and skirts had sculpted collars that made them appear far more provocative than they actually were if you managed to focus on the minimal amount of skin exposed. They were also in powerful colors that would draw an entire room's attention on whichever woman wore these.

She considered how the second one might look on her for a moment. No. Not quite her style. Perrin was right, these were constructed rather than the softer looks that Maria preferred.

In another booth lounged a pair of bridesmaids with their feet propped comfortably on the opposite bench seat, revealing Perrin's magnificent skill at draping and her understanding of a woman's body. They were in a shocking rainbow of color, broad stripes swirling about the mannequin forms. It should have been ugly, even grotesque, yet Maria could almost see herself standing beside three women so clad.

A clerk and a couple women were chatting comfortably in front of a triple mirror, one blonde and slender, the other Jamaican dark and bountifully curved. They were both trying on business suits, though that was perhaps the only phrase that connected the two garments. Wholly different designs and fabrics, but they bore the same clear punch of power. Not "I am a woman in a man's world," but rather "I am Woman! Watch out!"

"Maria!" Perrin came out of the back room and rushed over to give her a big hug. She still had her stark white hair, and her face was still unadorned, but she wore an emerald-green blouse and skirt that looked like a flapper's dress, if it had been made for a futuristic science fiction movie out of slick fabrics. She looked incredibly sexy and glamorous. She also looked as if she belonged to a far superior race and had just been beamed down to the Planet Earth.

"Come! Come!" Perrin dragged her through the doors into the back room. It had been the kitchen and was now set up with stylish raincoats on spatula-wielding mannequins, racks of colorful umbrellas dangled from above rather than copper pots and pans, and shoe-lined pantry shelves. She dragged Maria on through an open walk-in freezer lined with shelves of accessories and into her design space through a swinging door installed beyond the rear of the steel-clad cubical space.

"Go back there. Get naked." Perrin practically shoved her behind a classic Victorian changing screen that blocked off a corner. Its top was draped with half-a-dozen garments tossed negligently to dangle there.

"But—" Her attempt to protest was ignored. Maria had her coat off and was halfway to undoing her blouse before she came to her senses. "No. Wait. I came to talk to you."

"That's fine," Perrin came around the corner of the screen

and finished the job of removing Maria's blouse. "But I can't talk until I see this on you. No peeking."

Giving in, Maria finished undressing down to her underwear.

"I have your measurements from that dress I made for you a few months ago. So this should be close. You have such an amazing figure."

Perrin's running monologue made it impossible for Maria to interrupt, or even get her balance. In moments, she was standing with eyes closed as Perrin slipped a dress over Maria's head.

"At first I figured since this would be your first time, I should go all out."

"All out on what?" But Perrin ignored her question.

"Then I thought about you being such a classic beauty that I wanted to showcase that, so I decided simple and elegant. Keep your eyes closed, I just need to do some pinning here. It is the woman we want to really show off."

Maria bore up as well as she could, her head spinning wildly. It made it difficult to keep her balance and more than once Perrin had to steady her.

She had her suspicions as to what the dress was. Then was sure she was right. Perrin had said she'd make a wedding dress for Maria. Well, she wasn't ready for it, but she knew better than to try and stop Perrin when she was on a roll.

"Is this what you did for Jo and Cassidy?"

"You mean accost them in a dark alley and force an amazing dress over their heads with no warning at all?" Perrin mumbled around a mouthful of pins.

"Yes!" Maria felt terribly lightheaded as Perrin made subtle changes that caused the dress to shift and cling to her skin.

"Uh. Guess so. Never thought about it much. Cassidy not so much. She was the first of us to fall in love, I wasn't really ready for that. It was a real 'Duh!' moment for all of us when it finally happened. Jo?"

Perrin tugged on something that threatened to cut Maria in two, but then eased back off before she had a chance to complain.

"Absolutely. I mugged her outright. If you ever want to see your daughter-in-law-to-be all soft and gooey, it was the day I put her wedding dress on her. She wasn't even dating Angelo yet, though they were sweet on each other for months, but they hadn't figured even that out yet. I told her to never underestimate the power of a great dress. It seems that was enough."

Maria opened her eyes in surprise. Perrin was inspecting the dress' bodice critically. When she went to glance down, Perrin put a hand under her chin to stop her.

"Not yet."

Maria focused on watching Perrin's face as she worked. Critical consideration. An inordinate amount of talent focused on the problem of just what to do with Maria's chest.

Perrin tugged a little. "Oh, I know! No peeking!" And she was gone. She returned moments later with a gold chain and a piece of the sheerest fabric Maria had ever seen.

"I must be wearing more than that."

"Yes, you better, or not a single man in the whole place would be able to speak, including the minister. Now be quiet."

Maria stood and was quiet. She closed her eyes again, to resist the urge to peek, and enjoyed the slightly pampered feeling of Perrin bustling about her. So, Perrin had known that Jo should be in love, even before she was. Or knew that she was long before Jo knew it. Or… Maria sighed. This was all getting much too deep for her.

Perrin was like her son in that way. Angelo was a deep chef. His growing success was his combination of an exceptional palate, that she liked to think came from her, and an intense intellectual focus that was all his own. He built layers, depths, whole oceans of flavors that rose and melded into a satisfying whole without either disappointing or overwhelming.

Perrin did the same thing in fabric and clothing design. Deep design.

Maria wasn't deep, she just liked to cook. She liked flavors. Liked the juxtaposition of the unexpected with the tasty. So much of what she did was by intuition and testing, rather than figuring it out beforehand.

Perhaps that was the problem? Hogan had figured out that he was in love with her. And she'd been trying to figure it out as well. It wasn't how she cooked. Maybe it wasn't how she fell in love.

"Okay. Keep your eyes closed until we get to a mirror." Perrin's hands were steadying as she guided Maria forward.

She barely noticed as Perrin slipped high heels on her feet. Sandals.

"You can open them now," Perrin finished positioning her then stepped aside.

Maria opened her eyes.

She almost turned around to see who the mirror was reflecting before she realized that she'd been transformed. Her hair, always worn loose to her shoulders, was swirled atop her head. A simple gold chain adorned her neck. Then the dress…

The dress.

"Father, Son, and the Holy Ghost, Perrin."

It was the simplest of dresses. It was "the little black dress" that every woman had in their wardrobe. But there the similarities ended. Every curve, every seam traced a line of Maria's body. Curves enhanced, waist trimmed. A forty-seven-year-old body that looked twenty-five.

But it didn't just look younger.

It was a twenty-five-year-old's shape but with maturity,

elegance, even a sophistication that Maria had always known she lacked.

The skirt pleated, ever so slightly emphasizing without enhancing womanly hips, as if celebrating the son she had birthed.

It swirled just shy of her knees stating, "This woman still has great legs and the confidence to show them." The strapped-leather sandals were merely the capstone on that statement.

"But how…" She turned to view her profile. Maria hadn't looked this good since before she'd gotten pregnant, if then.

She turned the other way. No clearer how the magic had been done.

"You have such great lines, I just emphasized them," Perrin moved in and they looked at her reflection together. "Your neck is your standout feature. So, the black dress draws all attention to your beautiful skin. Rather than a plunging neckline, being slightly more covered up will slay Hogan and leave him desperate to see more."

Perrin held up the bit of sheer fabric. She'd done something to it. She slid it over Maria's wrist like a corsage. For some reason that bit of an accent worked, setting off the dark dress, making it clearly a celebration.

"And watch what happens when he finally slides the ring on." Perrin took a thin strip of gold ribbon and wrapped it around Maria's finger.

It caught the glimmer of the golden necklace and stood out ten times more than it would any other way. A black dress that not only showed off the bride within and acknowledged the woman, but also highlighted and celebrated the sanctity of the marriage vows and the purpose of the wedding.

"We'll dress Hogan in a white tux and tails. He'll fight it, but it will be perfect. When you dance in his arms, it will be beyond perfect."

Maria pulled Perrin into her arms.

"You are right. It will be."

Her instincts had known exactly what they were doing when they'd led her to Perrin's shop. The answer was there all the time, she just had to see it herself in the smile worn by the woman in the mirror.

CHAPTER 12

Hogan had been bemused by the instruction. So far, he'd been the one to set their plans, showing Maria a new Seattle, the one beyond her normal haunts of Pike Place Market and Pioneer Square. He'd been thinking to take her for drinks and dinner at the Space Needle; the food was good, but the view was spectacular. Or maybe up to the St. James Cathedral for a performance of Handel's *Messiah*. It wasn't St. Patty's in New York, but it was still lovely.

This time, she'd sent him a simple text. "Waterfront Park. Seven p.m."

So, here he sat on a park bench staring across the water at the site of their first date, the Seattle Great Wheel. Tonight it was lit like a red and green pinwheel, a giant swirling disk against the night sky.

It had been a week since he'd told Maria he loved her. It had simply been true, so he'd said it. Really not one of his smoother moves. For the hundredth time since, he wanted to kick himself, but it wouldn't make it any less true.

Since his declaration, she had been her usual, amazing self. Mostly. He would occasionally catch her watching him thoughtfully. As if he were a loose cannon that might go off without warning.

Actually, that wasn't fair. That was simply what he'd felt like. The most Maria showed was that perhaps she was a little quieter and more thoughtful than usual. But she was still the best companion he'd ever been with.

They talked, he'd never talked so much in all his life, and they both had a splendid time doing it. He was a corporate software engineer, she was an exotic, Italian chef. She was a great beauty and he was, well, Hogan Stanford.

And they'd made love. Since he'd been stupid enough to just blurt his feelings out like that, they had made amazing love. What had started as good sex, had become wholly incredible. Tender, gentle, sweet one moment, wildly passionate the next. Such fierce mood swings that it set them both to giggling and other times close to tears. Whatever they might each think or feel, their bodies were very happy together. He ached with need for her no matter how often they sated it. She claimed to be suffering from the same problem.

He would be patient. Honestly he would. Maybe with time, he could get over being such a doofus. Maybe.

"What are you thinking so deeply?" Maria stood only a few feet in front of him. She looked even more radiant than usual.

"Thinking of you, what else? You have taken over my brainpan. Wiped out my gray matter and filled it with endless, vibrant tapes of a woman who smiles back at me for reasons impossible to fathom."

Then she did just that. Smiled at him, soft and close. An intimate sharing.

When he continued to stare at her, she swirled slightly side to side as if showing off her coat. Her coat! Sky blue, long wool. And a hat more golden than the sun.

He sat bolt upright in shock.

"You! It was you that I saw from my window. All of it was you from the very start."

She nodded, "I almost fall down when you tell me about that. You fell in love with me from a dozen stories above without even knowing I was me."

"I did. That's because I'm a smart guy. Either that or insanely lucky." She'd said love. It was the first time she'd acknowledged that he loved her as if it were simply a fact. Which it was. He felt a ray of hope, but quashed it hard. *Always rushing things, Hogan. Just stay relaxed.* He told himself that often, and unsuccessfully.

In answer, she merely held out her gloved hand and tugged him to his feet. Hand in hand she led him south along the sidewalk, turning in at the Great Wheel. To his surprise she walked right by the ticket line, as if she merely wanted a closer look.

He offered to get them tickets, she just shook her head and led him forward.

At the loading gate, she produced a pair of tickets from her coat pocket.

The man signaled there'd be just a short wait. Though several gondolas were loaded ahead of them, they were still standing out in the cold. Not that he minded. Holding Maria's hand in his, smelling the soft scent of her upon the air, he'd be content to stand for hours and watch the bright lights of the Wheel and the Seattle waterfront.

"Here we go." She led him aboard the gondola. But it was different from the other one they'd been in a few weeks ago. It was trimmed in black instead of white. Rather than a long bench seat on either side, there were four armchairs. They looked deep and comfortable. It was also warm; this gondola had a heater. Christmas carols were playing softly in the background. He'd known there was a single VIP gondola on the Wheel, but had never given it further thought.

Maria pushed him gently into the seat opposite hers, so they faced each other knee to knee. With a friendly nod, the attendant locked them in and they were off.

How was he supposed to admire the view with Maria sitting directly opposite him? She opened her coat and set it aside. She wore one of his favorite red dresses and a thin gold chain.

"I haven't seen that before." He traced a finger lightly along the warm metal and cool skin. "It makes your neck look amazing."

She nodded at the compliment, but still didn't speak. Her smile was full of secrets, ones that he had learned she wouldn't be revealing until she was good and ready. Sometimes he could pester the answer out of her, but not when she smiled like that.

Then they swung out over the dock and he looked down in surprise. The floor was made of glass. He could see the steady stream of people in holiday attire, wandering along the pier. So many couples and families.

If he was ever going to have a regret, it would be that he hadn't had children. He and Vera hadn't wanted any, though it had taken him over a decade to realize that too was information. He and Maria had met too late in life and now there would be no children. Of course the thought of having a hormonal teenager running around the place when he hit sixty destroyed the image.

He looked again out of the gondola. It was like they were in a glass bubble floating above the city.

Maria handed him a bottle of champagne. It had been opened and capped. She held out a pair of wide-bottomed mugs. She didn't need to explain, flutes on a moving gondola were just asking for a spill.

So, they sipped champagne and watched the city as they rose into the sky. At the very top, Maria broke her long silence.

"This was for you, Hogan. For how you make me feel when you said that you loved me. Like a bubble floating above the city. Not knowing if I was safe, or about to float away. It should have been terrifying, but it was not. I want you to know that."

For a moment, he thought this was a speech about how it was over. But before the fear could even begin to form, she leaned forward and kissed him in a way that wiped that doubt aside. Deep, tender, lingering. By the time they parted, they had returned most of the way to the bottom.

"Twice more around," Maria said as they swung through the loading station.

As they rose once more, she began talking. She told him of her first passion, of her love for her son, of her being abruptly out of a job when the senior Morgans had retired six months ago. She'd told him of the events before, but never the emotions or details.

"There is another thing I want you to know, Hogan. They set me up very well in thanks for my years of service. Very well. I want you to know that because it is important that you understand, I am no interested in you for your money. I maybe as comfortable as you are."

Hogan hadn't even connected that. Vera had certainly cared a great deal about the wealth and status, just not enough about him to remain true to her vows. As with any corporate executive, he certainly hadn't helped matters by working so many hours, but neither had he cheated. He'd never even thought about that with Maria. He should have, but he hadn't. And now he didn't need to.

She freshened their glasses as the vista of Seattle and Elliot Bay once again lay far below them.

"There is one other thing you need to know about me, Hogan."

He tipped his mug toward her indicating he was listening.

"I love you so very much that I do not know what to do with all of the emotion inside me."

She took the mug before it could slip from his nerveless fingers.

"Yes, I am being very full of surprise too." She brushed her fingers along the chain at her throat.

"Really? You love me?" His voice, little more than a croak, reflected strangely off the gondola's windows.

"So very much, you wonderful man. Now, if I know you, Hogan, this would be the good time for you to pull that ring out of your pocket."

He almost asked how she knew; he'd only purchased it this morning. But then thought better of it.

Instead he recalled Perrin's words about Maria, "Scary smart."

Hogan did it right. He knelt upon the sky, the clear glass at the bottom of a gondola a hundred-and-seventy-five feet in the air, and asked her properly.

When he slid the gold band around her finger, it was the happiest he'd ever been in his life.

The third time around the Great Wheel, not a word was spoken, and three of the four seats remained empty.

CHAPTER 13

The air in Hogan's condo seemed to shimmer it was so filled with energy and amazing scents. The wedding feast was both sumptuous and bountiful—very Italian.

Maria was proud of Manuel and Angelo, they'd really outdone themselves. The food had poured forth from Hogan's kitchen in such abundance that it was impossible to credit even if the prep work had been done in the nearby closed restaurant. They'd served family style, a dozen heaped dishes arriving on great platters all at once.

The centerpiece was a trio of traditional Christmas *panettone* loaves, tall, cylindrical, and baked to a crunchy deep brown. Inside they'd be a soft yellow bread filled with candied orange and raisins.

There was a massive tureen of Natalini, macaroni and meatballs in a capon broth soup and a huge dish of sausage-filled Ravioli alla Genovese buried in Nora's Ligurian basil pesto. Henry had sent over a whole side of halibut to show he wasn't hurt at Maria falling in love with someone else and the boys had roasted it with fennel and baby potatoes. A chicken Marsala, a rack of lamb with an apple compote...the bounty spread far down the table and to Maria, every bit of it smelled like home. After a prayer of thanks and blessing, everyone simply dug in, drank, laughed, and made merry.

Maria and Hogan had decorated the Christmas tree in the living room together last night. It glowed and reflected off the night-dark windows. They'd also brought some of the family portraits from the Pioneer Square condo, the first but not the last to hang on the long wall behind the dining table.

The massive oak table, lit with a dozen candles, was covered with a festive cloth purchased for the occasion. Maria and Hogan sat at the table's head. Everyone was crowded together elbow to elbow. Christmas garlands and long streamers of red-and-green ribbons were laced among them. And a single streamer of white, black, and gold had been threaded through them all. For so they had been dressed for their wedding; the color of gold the single accent to reflect the bond of their promise to each other.

They had seen no reason to wait. They weren't twenty after all. The ceremony had been small, attended only by their closest friends who even now sat about them. Hogan had managed to arrange for them to wed at St. James cathedral, an intimate afternoon ceremony of as much beauty and simplicity as her wedding dress.

Perrin sat to Maria's right. She squeezed the girl's hand as she held her ring close beside her necklace to indicate how perfect it had been. Neither of them risked speaking, because they'd just start crying all over again.

"They're happy for you," Hogan's whisper tickled her ear.

"Should they not be?"

"No, it's not that. They're genuinely happy for you. Even your son congratulated me and gave me a manly hug right down to a thump on the back that might have dislocated a few vertebrae."

Maria looked about the table. Saw Russell once again

wielding his camera, picking his own wife out as she, Perrin, and Jo giggled over something together. Manuel and Graziella sat so close together that it was likely there'd be another wedding celebration soon. The rest of the restaurant staff squabbled and ate and teased down the length of the table. She'd have to remember to ask Russell for a few copies to place on the dining room wall.

"This we should do, often," Maria murmured to Hogan.

At his nod, she grabbed up her knife and clanged it on a glass, calling all of them to attention, quieting the gathering.

"My husband and I—" she whooshed out a breath. "*Mamma mia!* That is a surprising thing to say out loud."

Cassidy joined in her laugh and nodded knowingly. Jo nodded as well, but she was marrying in the spring and couldn't truly understand.

"We," Maria took the safer road. "We do no want this to be a one-time event. The restaurant is closed Mondays and Tuesdays. From now to forever, you are all invited to here for dinner every Tuesday evening. Hogan has—"

"We have," Hogan corrected her.

She leaned over to kiss his cheek. He turned enough to make it a far more serious kiss that elicited a round of applause and several catcalls. When she managed to get her breath back, she turned once more to face the gathering.

"My husband and I," it wasn't any easier to say the second time. "Have this glorious dining table. Every Tuesday it will be here we all are eating of dinner. You do not need to call, you just come whenever you can."

This time the applause didn't have the catcalls. She looked at Angelo. He placed both hands over his heart and then held them out open-palmed to her. A gesture she'd forgotten from his childhood. She silently returned her heart to him, as the table started debating next week's menu.

"You are my family." She could barely mouth the words,

managed them only loud enough for the three girls to hear. True to the rules, the four of them were all crying together.

Much later, after more food, tears, a quick cleanup, and many goodbye hugs, Maria was at last alone with Hogan.

They stood close beside the shining Christmas tree, the only light in the room, and looked out his…their condo window. The quiet Seattle waterfront stretched before them. Off to the left, barely in view, the very highest gondola of the now still Seattle Great Wheel glittered like a star shining in the night.

Hogan held her close from behind. His voice tickled as he whispered in her ear. "Love you, wife." Then he chuckled. "You're right, that is wonderfully surprising to say. I'll have to say it more often."

"I promise I'll never tire hearing you say it, my husband." Maria lay back against him and slid her arms over his where they encircled her waist.

"They're your children, you know. They all call you 'Mama Maria,' every one of them."

Maria sniffled and nodded, unable to do more.

"I guess that makes them my kids as well," Hogan laughed in surprise at his own words.

She looked up in time to see that slow smile, that she so loved, light up his face.

He took her hand and raised it to kiss her on the ring as if anchoring it in place forever.

"A Christmas table surrounded by *our* family. Who could ask for more?"

KEEP READING

Keep reading for an excerpt from book #4:
Where Dreams Unfold
And reviews are a HUGE help.
Thanks for joining my journey, Matt.

IF YOU ENJOYED THIS, YOU MIGHT ALSO ENJOY:

WHERE DREAMS UNFOLD (EXCERPT)

A WHERE DREAMS SEATTLE ROMANCE

*P*errin **Williams hung up** the dress bags and collapsed onto the tattered gray sofa in her design studio. Exhaustion still rippled through her in familiar waves. She felt both the dull ache and the immense satisfaction that typically coursed through her after an exceptionally long bout of clothing design, her favorite form of play.

The gentle light of the warm late-April-in-Seattle morning filled her boutique and design studio with a soft glow that made her want to just sprawl here and giggle madly. Somehow, against all odds, her life had brought her to work and create in this wonderful, safe space.

This time the exhaustion had been earned at the wedding of one of her two best friends. "Jo" Thompson had married Angelo Parrano at an event of grand proportions in the heart of the Pike Place Market.

Many of the Seattle elite had attended. More than a few had commissioned dresses from Perrin's Glorious Garb. Which elicited another giggle that might have been a chortle of self-satisfaction.

No one around yet to tell her if her tired brain had tipped

over the edge to gloating, so she let herself revel in the wonder of it all.

To see her designs flashing among the wedding crowd had filled her heart in a way that had left her speechless more than once last night. Because it was a Market wedding, after all, Jo was the new director of the Pike Place Market, the finest street musicians had added their music—including some great dancing music from the rolling-piano guy. The food was perhaps the finest Maximilien's had ever made. Perrin had put a giant sign on the kitchen door, "Angelo not allowed past this point." The groom, one of Seattle's most highly-acclaimed chefs, had it coming. Everyone, including Perrin, had made sure he was reminded of that sign often throughout the night.

The bride and groom had looked so beautiful dancing beneath the moonlight. They swayed together out on the patio overlooking Elliott Bay, a backdrop of scooting ferries and the brilliant glow of the ice-capped Olympic Mountains beyond. The couple had looked so in love. So happy.

Perrin shot to her feet and paced around the studio. She'd gone past tired and tipped right over into hyperactively awake. At some point soon she'd crash for a day or two, but not yet.

She unzipped the first bag. Jo's dress of shimmering pale blue cascaded forth. She'd have it cleaned and properly boxed before Jo and Angelo returned from a week in Hawaii. Neither of them had ever been there, and a week was all either of them could afford to be away at the moment. April was perfect weather in both Seattle and the resort on Kauai's eastern shore, especially known for relentlessly pampering its guests.

Perrin pulled Jo's dress in front of her and posed before the tall antique tri-fold mirror of beveled glass and dark oak. She turned on the lights, the early morning sun didn't reach into this corner of her studio. The pale blue had complimented Jo's Alaskan-dark complexion and flowing black hair. There had been no need for the dress to accent the curves, Jo's body had provided those perfectly.

Perrin tilted her head critically, and then had to roll it around a bit to loosen the crick from a serious lack of sleep. The dress wouldn't do at all on her own pale skin and slender frame. She hung it on the "to be cleaned" rack.

From the second bag she pulled out the bridesmaid dresses that she and Cassidy Knowles had worn. They had been as softly gold as the bride's dress had been softly blue. The gold had picked up highlights in the best man's suit that Perrin had dressed on Russell.

She'd also accented the mother-of-the-bride's dress with just a bit of the soft gold as well, which had made the photographs really pop. Russell had shared a few tips with her that only a professional fashion photographer would know. Seeing Eloise giving away her previously estranged daughter had brought tears to everyone's eyes.

Perrin sighed and hung the other dresses beside the wedding gown. Cassidy and Russell. Jo and Angelo. That left only Perrin without a man anywhere on the horizon. Part of her didn't want one.

"Avert!"

It was like some order from a space-captain's chair, "Evasive maneuver delta." "Avert!" It always made her smile, and because it was such a silly and simple thought it usually did track her away from thinking of her life prior to meeting Cassidy and Jo in college.

She didn't want a man because of the nightmare example of her family, but she also desperately did want one. One like Cassidy or Jo had found. The rough edges of Russell, the sensitivity of Angelo. And as long as she was making a list…

A knock on her door had her checking herself in the mirror: a simple light wool skirt appropriate for fall and a bright spring shirt topped with a summery sheer batik scarf. She was missing a season. Which one? Oh, winter. She really was tired, something to do with not having slept except for occasional catnaps in the last four or five days.

"WILSON. Please tell me this is one of your crazy jokes." Except the Director of the Emerald City Opera was not given to jokes, at least not practical ones. Bill Cullen glared at the display window of the fashion designer's storefront that Wilson had led him to. The stuff in the window was cute, urban. He guessed it would draw a woman passing by into the shop, just as well as a dozen other places that he seemed to pass every day. They cropped up, more dreams than solid basis in either business acumen or common sense. Then they went away and someone else moved in the next day with their hopes and dreams clutched tight.

He turned away and studied the neighborhood.

Wilson Jervis had dragged him into the heart of the Belltown area to meet a designer. The old brick building did nothing to inspire his confidence. After Pioneer Square, this was one of the oldest portions of downtown Seattle, just north of the business core. Most of the area had been rebuilt, turned into condos and ad-agency-slick small business fronts. She was on a block that had somehow been bypassed by the neighborhood's recent rejuvenation and gentrification.

Its age showed in many ways, darkened brickwork, cracks in the sidewalk. An abandoned tattoo parlor across the street with a "Half-off for Two" sign that might have once lured customers, but was now superseded by the "Out of Business" sign across the glass. Next to it, a small bike shop looked to be doing okay. Belltown wasn't dangerous the way Pioneer Square had been before its restoration, this part of it was just old.

"My wife found her. Trust me," was all the reassurance the

rotund icon of the Seattle theater scene offered. He'd been leading the Opera with a confident and mostly unquestioned hand for decades. He'd taken a small company on the verge of insolvency and turned it into one of the five largest opera houses in the U.S., and one of the most respected in the world.

All that still didn't make Bill trust Wilson about this. They were mounting a new opera and it was up to Bill as stage manager to see that it happened perfectly, or at least on schedule and near budget. It was his job to make sure that every piece from set design to costumes to lighting came together by opening night, only six weeks away. What they were doing in Belltown, too early on a Monday morning, was beyond him. Well, not totally beyond him.

Carlotta Gianelli had thrown one of her world-famous tantrums and stalked out yesterday to fly back to Milan and now they needed a costume designer who could perform a six-month miracle in only six weeks. Gianelli had burned up over four months and achieved nothing except some sketches that no one liked or could interpret.

He glared back at the shop as Wilson knocked again.

The glass door bore bold-colored lettering so close to graffiti that he could barely read it. Except he could. The "P" and "G" were actually oversized, ornate letters in the Victorian style. Perrin's Glorious Garb, the second two words attached to the same "G" were actually artful slashes that he recognized as a variety of fashion styles ranging over the last fifty years, somehow done so that they made a unified whole. What he'd almost dismissed as tacky was actually a deeply nuanced understanding of design.

He peered into the window. The shop was dark, but a light shone in back. He spotted a waif coming through the store toward them, silhouetted by the light behind and pulling on a hat despite the warm day.

"We're not open yet," she called through the glass but was

already unlocking the door.

She was dressed like some teenager that had been thrown bodily into a closet and crawled forth wearing whatever she fell against. She wore a form-fitting silk turtleneck of new-grass green, an unlikely mauve skirt that evoked autumn swirled in pleats about her calves, and a filmy batik scarf the red-orange of a summer sunset that looked as if it had attempted to throttle her. All mismatched and crazy, the unlikely ensemble somehow looked good on her in a way he didn't care enough about to attempt to fathom. She'd topped it off with a knitwear winter hat with earflaps and a ridiculous pom-pom pulled down over pale-blond hair that brushed her narrow shoulders.

Wilson introduced them and talked his way into the shop as easily as he'd talked Bill away from the San Francisco Opera four years before.

Adira's death had made Bill a single dad at thirty-three years old. His need to escape "their" city and the needs of their two children had been the biggest factor by far. But Wilson had not played that card. Instead, he'd offered a new and interesting job in a different city, leaving it to be Bill's own realization that such a change was exactly what he needed to do for both himself and his kids. Tricky s.o.b. To this day he still didn't know quite how that had happened.

Bill followed Wilson into the shop, letting the Director deal with the sloppily dressed clerk. The shop had been set up like a 1950s diner, all chromed metal and red leatherette. Mannequins sat in booths in a quirky mash-up of eras. A '20s flapper cozied up with a '50s greaser and a '40s housewife. Yet that wasn't what they were. The housewife's wide, white collar wasn't on the housewife dress, it was on the flapper's, and it distinctly accented the cleavage. The greaser actually sported the classic lines of a '20s linen suit, but sewn in denim and flannel.

He could hear the girl bubbling away at Wilson about something. Sounded like a chickadee mixed up with one of those small singing birds. Disconnected flighty bits that, even if gathered together, wouldn't really communicate much.

The next booth included Victorian brocade set in a modern blazer, and a gown design that would be formal enough for an opera opening night yet remained racy enough for the hottest club. Even studying the piece didn't reveal how the two distinct messages had been combined in a single garment.

He glanced over at the shop girl, wondering when the owner was coming in.

This girl was all arms and legs and nerves. Her slender build was only emphasized by her height. Fingers flashed out to emphasize points, her gestures were twice life size. She made a grand sweeping gesture which suggested she might be a dancer as well.

She had rolled out a short rack which bore a set of dresses, wedding and two bridesmaids, and was showing them to Wilson as he slouched next to a particularly voluptuous mannequin in a Wall Street business suit. Cutting a suit to a full-figured woman was hard, and she'd made the outfit pop; that it was in hot '50s poodle-pink wool only made it more so. Then he focused on the wedding and bridesmaid dresses. Exceptionally fine work, yet wholly inappropriate for the stage, as it was a masterpiece of subtlety. He'd bet that the clerk would look good in the gold one.

The Director had really lost it this time. All of these clothes were studies of craftsmanship and nuance. But they weren't costumes, especially not ones that would play to the vast three-thousand seat expanse of the ECO Opera House at Seattle Center.

"Where's the designer?"

"Why?" The woman pulled down her winter cap as if to shield herself.

"We're here to see her for reasons that wholly escape me." Up close the girl wasn't so much of a girl. She was a woman, long and sleek. Her hair a long, thick, pale blond that looked too substantial for so elegant a neck. She looked him nearly in the eye despite, he checked, bare feet.

The hat of garish orange wool, with ridiculous ear flaps, had been pulled down almost far enough to hide her eyes, but they shone brilliant blue past pale lashes.

"Why?" Her voice was soft.

"Why what?"

"Why do the reasons escape you?" There was a real "duh" tone to her voice as if he were the one being exceedingly dense and not the other way around.

"Wilson wants to hire her and I want to tell the woman to her face that there's no way on earth I'll work with her."

She regarded him with those bright blues for so long that he had to fight to not look away. There was a mind behind those eyes. And a force of personality all out of balance with the crazed attire and flighty first, second, and third impression.

"Boy, it's going to really suck being you."

"Why?"

"Because Director Wilson Jervis of the Emerald City Opera has just offered me the contract to design the costumes for *Ascension*, your next opera. And because it sounds like fun, I," she turned briefly to Wilson, "thank you Mr. Jervis, yes" then she turned back to him, "have as of this moment decided to accept. Perrin Williams at your service."

She held out a hand and shook his numb fingers strongly when he held them out in shock like a trained puppy.

She was right, it was going to really suck being him.

Keep reading.
Available at fine retailers everywhere:
Where Dreams Unfold

ABOUT THE AUTHOR

USA Today and Amazon #1 Bestseller M. L. "Matt" Buchman has 70+ contemporary and military romance novels, and action-adventure thrillers. Also 100 short stories and lotsa audiobooks.

Booklist says: 3x "Top 10 Romance of the Year" and among "The 20 Best Romantic Suspense Novels: Modern Masterpieces." NPR and B&N say: "Best 5 Romance of the Year." PW declares: "Tom Clancy fans open to a strong female lead will clamor for more."

A project manager with a geophysics degree, he's designed and built houses, flown and jumped out of planes, solo-sailed a 50' sailboat, and bicycled solo around the world…and he quilts. More at: www.mlbuchman.com.

Other works by M. L. Buchman: *(* - also in audio)*

Action-Adventure Thrillers

Dead Chef
One Chef!
Two Chef!

Miranda Chase
Drone*
Thunderbolt*
Condor*
Ghostrider*
Raider*
Chinook*
Havoc*
White Top*

Romantic Suspense

Delta Force
Target Engaged*
Heart Strike*
Wild Justice*
Midnight Trust*

Firehawks
MAIN FLIGHT
Pure Heat
Full Blaze
Hot Point*
Flash of Fire*
Wild Fire

SMOKEJUMPERS
Wildfire at Dawn*
Wildfire at Larch Creek*
Wildfire on the Skagit*

The Night Stalkers
MAIN FLIGHT
The Night Is Mine
I Own the Dawn
Wait Until Dark
Take Over at Midnight

Light Up the Night
Bring On the Dusk
By Break of Day
AND THE NAVY
Christmas at Steel Beach
Christmas at Peleliu Cove

WHITE HOUSE HOLIDAY
Daniel's Christmas*
Frank's Independence Day*
Peter's Christmas*
Zachary's Christmas*
Roy's Independence Day*
Damien's Christmas*

5E
Target of the Heart
Target Lock on Love
Target of Mine
Target of One's Own

Shadow Force: Psi
At the Slightest Sound*
At the Quietest Word*
At the Merest Glance*
At the Clearest Sensation*

White House Protection Force
Off the Leash*
On Your Mark*
In the Weeds*

Contemporary Romance

Eagle Cove
Return to Eagle Cove
Recipe for Eagle Cove
Longing for Eagle Cove
Keepsake for Eagle Cove

Henderson's Ranch
Nathan's Big Sky*
Big Sky, Loyal Heart*
Big Sky Dog Whisperer*

Other works by M. L. Buchman:

Contemporary Romance (cont)

Love Abroad
Heart of the Cotswolds: England
Path of Love: Cinque Terre, Italy

Where Dreams
Where Dreams are Born
Where Dreams Reside
Where Dreams Are of Christmas*
Where Dreams Unfold
Where Dreams Are Written
Where Dreams Continue

Science Fiction / Fantasy

Deities Anonymous
Cookbook from Hell: Reheated
Saviors 101

Single Titles
The Nara Reaction
Monk's Maze
the Me and Elsie Chronicles

Non-Fiction

Strategies for Success
Managing Your Inner Artist/Writer
Estate Planning for Authors*
Character Voice
Narrate and Record Your Own Audiobook*

Short Story Series by M. L. Buchman:

Romantic Suspense

Antarctic Ice Fliers

Delta Force
Th Delta Force Shooters
The Delta Force Warriors

Firehawks
The Firehawks Lookouts
The Firehawks Hotshots
The Firebirds

The Night Stalkers
The Night Stalkers 5D Stories
The Night Stalkers 5E Stories
The Night Stalkers CSAR
The Night Stalkers Wedding Stories

US Coast Guard

White House Protection Force

Contemporary Romance

Eagle Cove

Henderson's Ranch*

Where Dreams

Action-Adventure Thrillers

Dead Chef

Miranda Chase Origin Stories

Science Fiction / Fantasy

Deities Anonymous

Other
The Future Night Stalkers
Single Titles

SIGN UP FOR M. L. BUCHMAN'S NEWSLETTER TODAY

and receive:
Release News
Free Short Stories
a Free Starter Anthology

Do it today. Do it now.
www.mlbuchman.com/newsletter

www.ingramcontent.com/pod-product-compliance
Lightning Source LLC
LaVergne TN
LVHW091553060526
838200LV00036B/825